FACETAKER

I fed the coins in the slot – two pounds, a fifty – and waited. Clunk. One of the pounds clattered down into the Return slot. I licked it and pushed it back in. A click, like pinball, and the green light in the screen went red. Now. What should I do with the blood? I dabbed the single drop of it between the eyes of my reflection, like an Indian caste mark, and sat upright, my eyes on the line.

There was a pause, like firing squad victims must register, only they never get to tell you, do they? Flash. As I blinked, a green after-image shivered behind my eyes, then there was the red light again. Should I smile? Flash.

Before the third flash I thought: what if that's where Denzil dabbed his blood, in the very same spot? Flash. Did that make us blood brothers? Flash, it went again.

Have you read?

FACETAKER

Philip Gross

■SCHOLASTIC

Scholastic Children's Books,
Commonwealth House, 1-19 New Oxford Street,
London WC1A 1NU, UK
a division of Scholastic Ltd
London ~ New York ~ Toronto ~ Sydney ~ Auckland
Mexico City ~ New Delhi ~ Hong Kong

First published in the UK by Scholastic Ltd, 1999

Copyright © Philip Gross, 1999

ISBN 0 439 01232 5

Typeset by
Cambrian Typesetters, Frimley, Camberley, Surrey
Printed by Cox and Wyman Ltd, Reading, Berks.

10 9 8 7 6 5 4 3 2 1

Contents

Prologue

There's always one somewhere, in the corner of the precinct, on the station forecourt, anywhere that crowds pass by. Waiting. Day and night it stands there, glowing with a white light from inside. There's nothing to it, really – just an upright chrome and plastic box, with a camera in it in a place you can't quite see. There are larger-than-life pictures on the outside – square-jawed men, cute kids and winsome women – as if, for just £2.50 in the slot, that could be you. There is a small grey curtain you twitch across to hide you, like a confessional in a Catholic church. People go in there looking serious and anxious like that, too.

It's not tall enough to stand up in. Watch a grown man and you'll see him squirm in sideways, stooping. First, he'll have glanced a moment in the little mirror, pretending to be casual so he won't look vain. You'll hear the rattling sound as he winds down the seat, and you'll see his knees and feet beneath the curtain, shuffling as he adjusts himself, pats his hair, straightens his tie. Then he'll be strangely still, as if he's frozen in time; then there's a blue-white flicker. Lightning. He comes out, sheepish, glancing at the slot where the photos will drop. If you're waiting for your turn, he won't look you in the eye.

Day and night it waits there, glowing. People come at all hours. No one likes the pictures that it shows them, but they come — somehow they have to — all the same.

1

Denzil's Game

I'm trying to think when it was, the first time – the first time I noticed that Denzil had that special thing about him. You could call it power. Things would happen round him like they did round no-one else. At the time it seemed exciting; it set my nerve ends on edge. It's only afterwards, looking back, that I realize the feeling was fear.

We were friends, after all. And the first time I'm thinking of, it wasn't me he was frightening; it was Mr Pinkus. I was a bystander, one of the class, though I caught on to what was happening quicker than most of the rest. He was subtle, Denzil was. You've got to grant him that.

And Mr Pinkus? If ever there was a natural victim, he was. You could see it in his eyes. The moment he stepped through the door, before most of the class had even noticed him, he looked cornered. It wasn't that we were out of order, just a bit high, the way you are when you know the English teacher's off – a teacher that nobody likes – and it's Shakespeare again. We were chatting and pushing each other about a bit and joking, and then the door opened. There was Mr Pinkus looking ... well, I've got to say it: pink.

It was his skin: it had that slightly boiled look. He blinked too, several times, as he looked around the classroom. You could see the pinkness of his scalp right through his thin white hair.

"Hello, sir." It was Denzil who spoke first, and it seemed polite – just a bit too polite to be true, but he smiled as he said it, and Mr Pinkus looked relieved and gave a bit of a smile in return.

"Uh, I understand Miss Stokes has set you work to get on with," he said.

Someone muttered something at the back, and Mr Pinkus jerked round. "Pardon?" he said and blushed. That's what gave Denzil his cue. Mr Pinkus's hearing wasn't too good these days; he missed things, and felt bad about it. He was a couple of years from retirement and you could see the younger members of staff thinking that the time couldn't pass too quickly.

"Ben said: *Yes she did, but she didn't explain it*, sir." Denzil spoke loud and clear, and Mr Pinkus's eyes were drawn to him. What a helpful boy, you could see him thinking. Looking back now, there was something just then in the way that Denzil nodded slightly as he smiled…

"Could you explain it to us, sir?"

"Oh…" Mr Pinkus said. "It's not my subject…" Mr Pinkus was Religious Studies. My mum told me later that he'd been a vicar once, but found it stressful so he turned to teaching. Little did he know.

"Please, sir?" said Denzil. I looked at the worksheet we'd been left. *A Midsummer Night's Dream*. "What is the dramatic effect", it said, "of Oberon telling Puck to make Titania fall in love with Bottom?" At the back of the class, some people shifted restlessly. For clarity, the question scored about two out of ten. It was the kind of question we could leave till Miss Stokes came back next week, then tell her we hadn't been able to do it because we didn't understand. If Pinkus went and explained now, we'd have to do it.

"Shut up, Denzil," whispered Lisa. Lisa was queen bee in our class, the one at the centre of the biggest group of friends, and what Lisa said went. Denzil was new, and in nobody's gang, but he gave her a straight look, not aggressive, just sort of calm and controlled. *I know what I'm doing*, it said. And – this is what I mean by *power* – Lisa let it go.

"Uh… 'What is the dramatic effect…' " Mr Pinkus started reading. Jase in the back row sniggered when he got to "Bottom". There was a moment when the others could have started too, but Denzil cut in right away.

"Do you think she means," he said, "What-is-the-effect-on-Puck-of-Oberon-telling-him-to-do-it, or does she mean it's-worse-for-Titania-because-Oberon-told-Puck-to-do-it-instead-of-doing-it-himself, or…?"

"Slow down," said Mr Pinkus. "That sounds like an intelligent question. I think you should all take notice…"

So Denzil went on. He looked serious. At first people fidgeted but one by one they fell quiet, as even the slowest ones got the message from the way Denzil was speaking. Loud. And. Clear. *E-nunc-i-at-ing* perfectly for Mr P… Something was going on. It was a performance of some kind and everyone from Lisa to Jase tuned in to listen, wondering what it would be.

Denzil was clever, you sensed it, though in the months he'd been there he hadn't let on much. He'd come from a school where they were big on Drama, and he seemed to be talking sense, using words like "dramatic irony". It was sort of touching to watch Mr Pinkus leaning forward, smiling, being grateful to Denzil for not showing up the fact that he hadn't read the play for forty years. Then Pinkus was leaning forward just a little further, and a little further, frowning so the skin between his eyebrows furrowed. And I realized that Denzil's voice was getting, very slowly, quieter…

I've got to say one thing: no one hated Mr Pinkus. He was a harmless sort of man, mild, quite nice even, on a good day. He might have been good as a vicar. He looked in some sort of pain now, as Denzil took the volume down and down, keeping his eyes on Pinkus' all the time. And just as the man was about to say "I'm sorry, I can't hear you," suddenly Denzil took the volume up again.

"Is that right, sir?" said Denzil, very clearly, and stopped.

Mr P looked round, flustered. "Uh, would anyone else care to comment?" he said. No one met his eyes, but Lisa twigged. Her hand went up.

"Please sir," she said distinctly, and began. I forget what she said – she wasn't as good at it as Denzil – but in a minute or two she caught Denzil's eye, he nodded, and she started slowly fading, until she was mouthing as if she was talking loudly but someone had their finger on the volume and… Mr Pinkus looked rattled. He sat down, awkwardly. Under the pinkness, he was going pale.

I know what you'll say, if you're kind. You'll say: don't blame yourselves for what happened next. You can't expect fifteen-year-old kids to understand how a man in late middle age, just on the brink of old, feels when he knows he's losing it. Just a couple of years to hold out for his pension, and he's wondering if he can make it. You can't expect kids like us to guess that he's been bluffing for years, trying to hold on to his dignity, but there are nights he wakes up sweating. Of course you can't ... except that somehow Denzil knew. He had an instinct for it. He saw people's soft spots as if they had targets painted on them. I think that was what happened in that moment when he nodded as he smiled.

Denzil took over from Lisa. He was the star. We'd seen him in Drama and we knew that he could improvise. Maybe that's all he ever did, really. Miss Stokes had lost her cool once when she gave him a script and, in the middle of page three, the rest of the cast realized they couldn't find any of the words he was speaking. "So you think you can improve on Shakespeare?" she said, in her lemon-sucking voice.

"That's what we always did at Darkington," Denzil said. "It's called Creative Response." Darkington was this alternative school he'd been at, all performing arts and self expression, before he landed back here in the suburbs when his parents split. If you believed the stories, Darkington was a school where the kids voted on who'd take assembly that morning, and what religion it would be.

"Well, you're not at Darkington now," Miss Stokes had said, curdlingly, and Denzil had nodded meekly and read on, word perfect but somehow in a tone of voice that made every line mean the opposite of what it said.

So Denzil could improvise. And Mr Pinkus? He was hooked. Outside, across the car park, in the main road, there were roadworks going on. Every now and then a pneumatic drill would start up, and that's where Denzil's skill showed. Each time the background noise went up, he upped the volume; when it stopped, he eased it back. If there'd been birds out there, I can't help feeling they'd have got the drift and joined in too. That's how it was, with Denzil.

Mr Pinkus was twitchy now, and his forehead was glossy with sweat. Every now and then he put his hand to his ear. His eyes were sort of jerky, looking back and forth for clues or help. "I ... I'm sorry..." he started once, but we ignored him. Then the *coup de grâce*...

Outside, the drill stopped suddenly, and the whine of the compressor cut out too. At that second, Denzil glanced round like a conductor, and we were all putting our hands up, mouthing as if we were calling out, but silent. Mr Pinkus staggered to his feet, with both hands to his ears, and stumbled backwards. His chair tipped back and for an instant it hung there, and I really thought that time and sound had stopped, then crash... And with immaculate timing, Denzil and a few others were on their feet, at full volume again, calling "Sir? Are you all right, sir?"

Mr Pinkus did not answer, he just turned and bolted.

There was a hush, and we looked at each other. Outside in the corridor, quietly at first, someone was sobbing. It started as a high-pitched whimper, like a child. "Someone go and look," said Lisa, after a while. I was nearest the door.

I wished I hadn't. Mr Pinkus had his face in his hands as if it had come loose and he had to hold it on. As I peered from the doorway he looked up and saw me, and he groaned. He blundered off down the corridor, crying as he ran.

It was ten minutes before the head came in, and she looked rattled too. We braced ourselves for a bollocking but it never came. "Mr Pinkus..." she said in a grave voice, "has been taken ill. Rather upsettingly ill..."

There was a pause. She looked at Lisa. "He just ran out, Miss," said Lisa, big-eyed. "Will he be all right?"

"I hope so," said the head. "He's just been ... under a lot of stress, that's all." By the end of the day, though, "breakdown" was the word everybody was using. There'd been an ambulance at Reception and all of Year Seven, on the ground floor, had stories of how they'd heard someone shouting and sobbing in the corridor. A few of them went home quite upset, and next morning in assembly the head had to do a whole thing about mental health problems and how they can strike anyone at any time. "I think we should all remember," she wound up, "what a good and kind man Mr Pinkus was, and hope he can be back with us soon." But we all noticed that she said *was*. Several of us glanced at each other sideways, and especially at Denzil, but he didn't glance back. To any outsider, he'd have looked like a good boy, listening. A lot of the time, in class, he'd have a slightly bored look some teachers found annoying. Right now, I couldn't see any expression on his face at all.

Maybe that was it: the first time that he frightened me. If there'd been a flicker of anything – he didn't have to be ashamed or guilty, just embarrassed would have done – he'd have been just like the rest of us, thinking what a smart game it had been, pushing the man to the edge, until he was over. You never know, do you, how close that edge is? Then it's too late.

I should have hated Denzil. It was true: Mr Pinkus was a kind man, really. In the wrong place at the wrong time, isn't that what they say? He'd been defenceless, that was all. I should have hated Denzil for it, but I didn't. I felt my heart beating faster. It was like football, when you watch the other side's striker slip through your defence so smoothly and skilfully, not a sign of effort, that when the ball smacks home you've got to cheer. Just for the style of it. Denzil had style. Whatever else you say about him – and everyone thinks they've got something to say about him these days – you've got to admit he had style.

And let's be honest, we forgot about Pinkus in a week or two. That's the sad bit, and a kind of warning too. If I'd really thought about it then, maybe all the things that happened later wouldn't have. You never know how close anyone is to the edge, as I said. Least of all your friends and you.

That's all easily said. You must remember: he had style. And for people like me, who do the right things and work hard and no one looks at them twice, that counts for so much. Besides, Denzil never *made* anyone do anything. Whatever happened, I guess we must have wanted it to.

2

All Change

The station was a cast iron vault. Look round on ground level and you're in the present, with red plastic signs and automatic glass doors that hiss open with their electronic eyes. Look up, you could be in a burned-out cathedral.

Denzil needed a photo taken, some ID or other, so we walked past after school. This was a couple of months after the Pinkus affair. We'd spent a bit of time together. He didn't have friends exactly, not a group of them. He'd just stride into school from a slightly different direction from everyone else, in that long black coat with lots of buttons, kind of Seventies retro-style. He wasn't unfriendly – certainly not shy. Some days he'd just walk in and sit down, smiling very slightly, tapping his fingers as if he had a Walkman you couldn't see. He'd sit back a bit and watch the rest of us through slightly hooded, sleepy-looking eyes. First time I asked him what he was thinking: "Oh," he said, "just observing." People have tried to say he must have been lonely, left out, but that doesn't make sense to me. If Denzil came in and sat down on his own, you started to feel it was everyone else who was left out. That was the power. I couldn't imagine being like that, not caring what anyone thought of me. I wished I could. After a while I'd drift over to him, and if he felt like it he'd let me in on what he was thinking. With Denzil, that was being friends.

As we entered the station concourse there was a noise so loud it hurt. On platform one the InterCity was powering up in a haze of blue diesel steam. It started as a whine and it built to a roar, like fifty pneumatic drills in competition. It's a big station, a junction, and half of England seems to change there, passing through. Up among the iron girders, there's a century of smoke and soot, full of echoes and feathers and bird lime and an emptiness that's always there, looking down on our small hurrying lives the way we might look at an ant's nest.

The noise shook loose about a thousand pigeons in a panic. Then the brakes hissed off and the train started slowly, with a noise like metal grinding on a lathe. For a time we couldn't talk or think, so we watched the carriages slip past, getting faster, and there were faces framed in every window, staring out like clothes-shop dummies. Masks; I suppose there were people inside them, but how could you ever know who they might be?

"Damn," said Denzil. "There's somebody in there."

The photo booth was pushed back in the corner of the concourse, between an industrial-sized grey rubbish bin and a pile of rubbish that was meant for it but had missed. From the whitish plastic walls a more-than-life-size woman's face gazed out with blue eyes and butter-blonde hair. The more I looked at her, the more unnerving her too-perfect teeth became. Behind it, the brick wall was the colour of dried blood and ashes. Beneath the hem of the little grey curtain, we could see a bit of raincoat and some feet. That's all I registered at first glance, and Denzil was already passing the time by felt-penning out one of the photo girl's front teeth, so we laughed about that for a bit. It was several minutes before we noticed that the woman in the booth didn't seem to have moved at all.

Two, three minutes, that's all it should take. And Denzil didn't like queuing. The reason he walked everywhere, with that long-legged lope of his, leant slightly forward, was that no way, he said, would he ever stand in line and wait.

"Hey," he said suddenly. "Some legs!" I looked

under the curtain and grinned ... then winced. Poking out from the hem of the grubby grey coat were two hugely swollen ankles, wrapped in surgical bandages, round and round. The dressing couldn't have been changed for weeks, it was so mud-stained and fraying. In the creases of it, brownish blood or pus had leaked, then caked and dried.

Alice the Bag. She was a local feature around the station, along with the down-and-out kids with thin whispery voices, in all kinds of accents. They came and went. Then there was VI, the hulking moon-faced one who didn't look like a beggar at first because he wore a jacket and a tie, a different tie each day. "Excuse me, spare a copper for a cup of tea?" was his opening line, or sometimes, "Excuse me, but we've lost our train fare home, me and my brother..." The voice was polite but not quite right, a child's voice in a grown-up body. He was slow. The village idiot, Denzil called him once, VI for short. But Alice was queen of the patch. You saw her trudging slowly, hunchbacked, or stopping to lash a new find to her broken trolley. I'd seen her hundreds of times, but not from this close. You didn't, not if you could help it. She was famous for her smell.

"Yech," I said. "Go in there after *her*, you'll have to burn your clothes when you get home."

I looked again, at those legs. I couldn't help it. The really sick thing was that at their ends, crammed on over the bulging bandages, were carpet slippers, flip-flops with still just a trace of pink fun-fur.

"She's asleep," said Denzil. "The old bat's having a snooze." It was true. Five minutes at least we'd been there, and you could see from the way her knees had lolled apart that she'd slumped back. I was surprised we couldn't hear her snoring.

"Hey," I said, "do you think she needs a passport? Where do you think she's going?" For a horrible moment I imagined her prettying herself up in there for the photo, going coy and girly, fluffing up her thinly frizzed grey hair. I looked at the slot in case a strip of four of her slipped out, glossy and wet, but there was nothing there.

Denzil was pacing. "Come on," he muttered. "I haven't got all day." He gave a loud excuse-me cough. No response.

"You could give her a nudge," I said.

"Huh. After you."

"No thanks."

"OK, so we knock." He banged. It must have been loud in there, an inch or two from where her head must be, through the thin plastic wall. She did not stir.

"Oh, leave her," I said. She was getting a wink of sleep in a dry place; we couldn't really begrudge her that. I didn't like to think where she slept by night, in her carpet slippers.

"No way," said Denzil, not to her. "I want my

photos. OK, Mr Nice Guy. You wake her up nicely. How about a morning cup of tea?" And he jerked the little curtain back.

"Excuse me," I said. No reply. I held my breath, leaned in and tugged her sleeve.

It happened slowly, in stages. First her arm slithered off her lap and flopped at her side. As I jumped back, the weight of it overbalanced her and she began to crumple towards me. She wedged in the door for a moment, she was so wide with her head lolled forward, then it rolled the other way, and she slithered on out, with a soft thump on the pavement. She rolled over halfway and lay, her face up and her feet still twisted at an angle in the booth. Her mouth lolled open, with a few grey teeth here and there in the gums. Pushed forward in among them, I could see her tongue. Her eyes were open and dull, and for the first time in my life I knew that I was looking at a real person, really dead.

For half an hour it was a drama. Just like on TV, there were blue lights and sirens, and the paramedics came rushing up in their green and yellow jumpsuits. Once they'd seen her, though, they slowed down; they made one or two checks and switched from Hurry into Tactful mode. They started hushing people away; "There's nothing to see," they said. There was no way Alice could be anything but dead. The small crowd that had gathered moved back but did not disperse, and you could feel the little thrill run through them when the paramedics pulled the stretched blanket up to cover her face.

"You spoke to her?" said the policewoman, once the ambulance had moved off. "Loudly?"

I shook my head. Once Kate, my kid sister, had a hamster, and we tried to wake it up when it was hibernating. It sort of yawned and stretched and got itself almost upright, then suddenly it gave this horrible little shudder and fell over and died. It's the strain on the heart, the vet said, if you wake them up too quickly.

"That was all?"

I nodded. I wasn't going to say I had actually touched her. I could feel it on my fingers still, the greasy mac. I didn't want to sniff my hand in case I smelt her. The moment I got home, I'd run hot soapy water and I'd scrub it hard.

"The truth, the whole truth and nothing but the truth?"

It was evening. We were back at my place, and we'd retreated upstairs to my room. If Mum had said "Dead! How dreadful…" one more time I'd have screamed. Upstairs, I poked around to find a CD but nothing I picked up seemed right.

…*And nothing but the truth?* Denzil was looking at me sideways with that hint of a smile.

"It didn't matter," I said. "She'd been dead for ages. They said so."

"Maybe," he said, deadpan. Then he burst out laughing. "You should see yourself! I hope you never commit a real crime. It's like a neon sign on your face saying: Guilty!"

"It's not funny," I said. "It's horrible. It's sad."

"Yeah? You were fond of her, were you?"

I said a rude word.

"Well? So why's it sad?" When I didn't have an answer, he seemed to lose interest, as he often did, and turned away.

"Hey," he said, turning back suddenly. "Want to know something really funny? Funny-peculiar, I mean... Something rather important that *I* didn't tell them?" He leaned back in his chair and tapped his nose.

"What?"

He made a thinking sort of face.

"Tell me!" He had me hooked as sure as he'd had Mr Pinkus.

He didn't say a word. He smiled, then reached into his shirt pocket and lifted out something, carefully, as if it was fragile. For a moment he kept it cupped in his hand.

"Be careful with this," he said. "It's special." I held my two hands out flat and he laid the little card strip in them. It was from the photo booth.

"A bit of all right," he said, "isn't she?"

All right wasn't the word for it. Looking out at me, in four exposures, was one of the loveliest faces I have ever seen. She wasn't pin-up glamorous – much subtler than that – a heart-shaped face framed by black hair with wide black eyes. She was dark, dark enough to have just a hint of something further east than Indian, like Thai or Balinese. The mouth and the eyes were as neat as if they'd been outlined in pencil and at their corners was a slight tweak, like someone teasing very slightly, with a joke she could not share. No joke, though: there was something wistful way back in the hidden inner spaces of those eyes.

If that was Denzil's girlfriend... But no – he wasn't the kind of handsome that makes girls go giggly in the changing room. You know how some people have the kind of face that looks a bit too grown-up even when they're young, as if they'd borrowed one from their uncle? Sometimes I've looked in the mirror and thought: it's perfectly OK, my face, but so what? We've all seen films where the bad guy, Mr Big, is ugly and completely surrounded by beautiful women. You'd like to think it's just money, but deep down you know there's more to it. Denzil wasn't ugly, but it wouldn't have mattered if he'd had an eyepatch, warts and scars. Whatever it is, that kind of power, Denzil had it, as simple as that.

If that was Denzil's girlfriend I was going to eat myself with jealousy.

"Who is she?" I whispered.

"Don't know."

"Pardon?"

"I don't know. It came from the photo booth. What with the police and the paramedics, no one else was looking. I just saw them lying in the slot..." He paused, and his eyes held me, daring me to say *"So what?"*

"And..." he stretched the moment nearly to breaking point. "And they were still damp. You know what that means? Think about it."

How long does it take for these things to process? Five minutes? We'd been standing outside for much longer than that. And Alice? She could have been there half the afternoon.

I looked up at Denzil. He was smiling, nodding very slightly, the way he did when he decided what to do with Mr Pinkus. That was the start, and he knew it. He couldn't have known, even him, where it would end, this game of his.

3

De-facing

"Like a flashbulb," Denzil said. He had this way of saying things, dropping words out of the blue so at first you couldn't guess what he was on about. "That's what it's like when you die. Like: all the energy inside you burns up in one go. Zap. It's got to leave some kind of trace."

"Hold on," I said. "Slow down."

He didn't slow down. He was up on his feet now and pacing. Suddenly my room seemed very small. I've seen jaguars in cages at the zoo like that, stalking end to end then round with a swish of the tail, eyes burning. He stopped, just as suddenly, at the window and leaned up to it, his face and its reflection almost touching as he gazed at nothing outside in the dark. "Yes!" he breathed to himself. Then he turned back. "Don't you see?"

Intense: that's the word for Denzil's face. Not a pin-up, like I said, not the kind of girl-boy looks that half the film stars have these days, but girls noticed him, all right. You could see them, in spite of themselves, keep glancing sideways at that face. There was something about it that was … well, just a bit too much. The eyebrows were too dark, the arch of his nose too strong and bony, and his forehead just a bit too high, with the hair cut straight across it – straight beneath his cheekbones too, like sideburns that gave him an an old-fashioned look. If you'd seen him in a Victorian album, in a high collar, or in a painting from Henry VIII's time, with a ruff, he wouldn't have been out of place. And his eyes… Right now, they were glittering and dark, like water under a bridge.

"Doppelgängers…" He was speaking quickly. "Someone dies. Five hundred miles away, somebody sees them, just like that. When they check up later…" A theatrical pause. "They find it was the exact moment of death." He was an actor, like I said, an improviser, and the timing came naturally. Once after Drama at school, when he'd been brilliant as an abused, abandoned orphan, the teacher came over, concerned, to make sure that it wasn't really true.

"Doppel-thingies?" I said. "Ghosts? Don't start on that stuff…"

"Not ghosts. I mean *energy*. You know when stars burn out, they fade and fade and then, just at the very last moment, they flare up. Go supernova. What if it's like that when you die?"

"Sorry," I said. "You've lost me."

He gave a frisk of impatience. "Just imagine. If you had a camera, just at that moment…"

"That's sick," I said.

" …or a photo booth."

"And two quid fifty in the slot?"

"It doesn't matter. The film's there ready. If somebody's image can go five hundred miles, it can get through a bit of plastic."

"Hold on," I said again. With half a gram of sense I'd have said: *You're just making this up.* Knowing him he'd have grinned and said: *Fair cop.* Even if he wasn't. But I didn't say it. This was getting good; I felt a shiver up my skin. The last thing I wanted was for him to say it wasn't true.

"Are you talking about … these?" I said. The face in the passport strip was gazing up at me, four times over, with those secret, deep dark eyes.

"I'm talking about Alice."

"You're welcome. I'd rather have this one…"

"No!" he cut in, sharp. No joking. "What if … what if that *is* Alice?"

"What?"

"Or was. There was nobody else in that booth. You saw for yourself. So what if that *was* Alice, years and years ago?"

I squinted my eyes. Could I imagine that sleek black hair gone grey and frizzy? Those delicate features lost in wrinkles and pouches of fat? That mouth with its teeth gone, folding in on its gums? For a moment I could see the princess in the picture blurring, falling into hard times and disintegrating into old age, into Alice... No! That Alice had been a girl once, young and even pretty, was a thing I didn't want to think. If that girl could be Alice, then it – old age, falling apart – could happen to anyone.

"Or," said Denzil. "Maybe it's what she *dreamed* of being? Imagine that." I thought of Alice, curled up in some doorway with her bags piled round her, snoring, while behind her eyelids she was in another world, and looked like this.

"Or maybe she thought she was, in her pretty pink slippers. She was crazy, after all." He shrugged. "Weird things, photographs," he said abruptly and lifted them out of my hands. When he'd gone, I closed my eyes and there was the girl's face, burned on my retina. It was like he'd said: one moment is enough, flash, and there's an image printed in your brain.

* * *

"You'll never guess who I saw," said Mum brightly. Some family breakfast times, when everyone else was feeling dull and getting on with it, she'd be like this, as if it was the extra vitamins we needed to start the day with. Snap, crackle and pop. I hoped it was aimed at Kate, who was deep in her boy-bands magazine, or Keir, who was dibbling his spoon in his porridge, or Dad, who was there but somewhere else, if you know what I mean. But no, she was looking at me.

"Sarah!" she said. "You used to be fond of her, didn't you?"

Kate looked up. "Sarah? You mean cousin Sarah? Really? Her and Jon?"

"No," I said. "We used to play together when we were little kids. You know, younger than you."

"Ah, a man with a past," said Kate, through cornflakes, and was back in her magazine.

"Sorry," said Mum as I got up from the table. "I just wanted to take your mind off … you know, yesterday." We weren't to mention *death* in front of Keir. He was too young to understand, said Mum. "You mustn't brood on it," she said. "Promise me you won't."

"Sure. Thanks, Mum. If I really want to depress myself, I'll think of Sarah." It was a weak sort of joke, the kind of dig boys my age make at girls all the time, and Mum made the effort to smile. I often wonder if she thought back later and blamed herself. If she hadn't mentioned Sarah when she did, I might never have thought about her and the photograph game. Though in hindsight the memory was lying in wait for us, just waiting to be found.

Funny things, photographs, Denzil had said, the night before. That was when he'd given up on me asking my sensible questions, not keeping up with the way his ideas took off, sort of wild but free. He'd gone home not long after, and he left me feeling … well, just dull. Now Mum had reminded me of something. I went upstairs and rooted through my cupboard. Yes, pushed right to the back, in a cardboard box full of old holiday postcards and football stickers and cereal-packet free gifts and other stuff too ancient and embarrassing even to put in the bin … there it was. A passport-size photograph, a bit creased and faded. If you'd seen it you'd have said *Is that your Grandad?* You'd have had to look quite closely to spot the subtle dabs of Tippex and the fine-line felt pen, and even closer before you realized that the old man in the photograph was me.

It had been one of those family Christmases, the kind you try to forget, when Sarah and I did the photograph game. My mum and dad had got the whole tribe gathered that year, and the uncles and aunts were talking new cars and mortgages. All the little ones were penned in the lounge with their new toys and the Snowman video, and somewhere in the middle, neither one thing nor the other, were Sarah and me. She was thin and awkward, with little round glasses, and I was … well, a twelve year old version of me. We didn't have to be friends; we were allies. It was going to be hard work, though; she was shy.

The breakthrough came when we stumbled on the photos. Four different exposures of me. They were all pretty bad but the least worst had gone on the passport. I'd stuffed the other three away out of sight in the cupboard and it was while we were searching in there for something, anything, that Sarah and I could play with, they slipped out and landed at her feet.

"Is that you?" she said.

"Who do you think it is? Arnold Schwarzenegger?"

"It could be," she said. I stared. She'd never spoken above a whisper till now. "Have you got felt pens?" she said, and a minute later she was at work, making small adjustments. A bit more chin here, and a touch of stubble. There, a bulge of muscles where my shoulders dropped away. She gave the corner of my mouth a sardonic tough-guy twist.

"Hey," I said, "that's really lifelike." But suddenly she blushed.

"It doesn't feel right," she said. "Drawing on a

real person. I usually do it with famous people in the paper. That's different. I did one of Tony Blair, how he'll look when he's grown up. Sorry..." She was shy again. "That's my mother's joke, not mine."

"Great. Do one of *me* when *I'm* grown up."

"That's hard," she said, and looked at her feet. "I'd have to look at you."

"I'm used to it. You know, the press, the paparazzi..." She smiled weakly.

"Keep still," she said. "I've got to work out where the lines will be." It was odd, watching her do it. She would glance down at the photo-face then up at me, then back, and her fineliner tip would do a little scribble. She didn't meet my eyes, not even when she was looking at them, and I wondered what she really saw. Was it my face, or me? Just as I caught myself thinking that question, and wondering what it meant, she suddenly looked up. "There!" she said, and held it out so I could look into his face, this forty-year-old man who was, and wasn't, me.

"I need some white stuff," she said. "I can do you older. You'll have to have a beard."

"No way. I wouldn't be seen dead in a beard."

"You might. I'll do you at ninety." And she did. At some point in all this we started giggling, though it might have been Mum's cooking sherry, left over from the trifle. I'd smuggled us up a wine glass each. "Sir Jon Westman," she said as we both admired it. "Grand Old Man Of … what?"

"Rubbish. He looks like a tramp."

"Have it your own way." A quick doodle, and there was a bent cigarette end in his mouth. She picked up the red fineliner and gave it a glow at the tip. Then she reddened up his nose a bit and gave him bloodshot eyes. "Hey, don't," I said, but I was laughing. That's when Auntie Bea came in.

"My God," she said. "Where did you get that?" She looked closer. "You horrible children. What are you doing?" Sarah looked at me; I looked at Sarah. When we looked at Auntie Bea she was quivering, pale in the face but her eyes were full of tears. "How dare you?" she said. "It's wicked – defacing a picture of poor Uncle Gilbert. And he only died last year."

"Nice one, Jon," said Denzil. "I thought you said you had no imagination." (I said that sometimes, when he tried to get me to join in and improvise.)

"Who needs imagination? This is *true*."

"Better still. Who is this Sarah?"

"Just a cousin," I said. "I haven't seen her for years. Not since that Christmas." Denzil raised his eyebrows. "It was bloody," I said. "Aunt Bea made a real stink. It spoiled everybody's Christmas. Sarah got hauled off in tears, and everyone said it was my fault, somehow."

"Call her," Denzil said. "I want to meet her."

"It was only a game." I was wriggling. Denzil fixed that steady look on me.

"Call her," he said. "If you're not making it up – you aren't making it up, are you? Well, then, maybe there's something special about this Sarah of yours."

"She's good at drawing, yes…"

"No." He was losing patience. "I mean something *special*." That was a word he used a lot. It meant the opposite of ordinary, boring, just like all the others. It meant worth bothering with. If Denzil didn't think you were special, you were nothing. "Call her," he said. So that was what I did.

4

Two Dogs

I cut through the car park, where it said No Public Right Of Way. The sun glinted on ranks of blind windscreens. In between, the ground was cinders, with gouts of purple weeds coming through. No one in sight; it was eerie how ten thousand commuters could vanish in an hour every morning, leaving the place as empty as if it had been hit by a neutron bomb. Now and then there was the echoey crackle of the announcer's voice from the station beyond. I could slip through the wire and be there by the back way five minutes quicker than walking round on the road. I wasn't late but I was in a hurry. For some reason I wanted to be there first.

The station buffet, half past ten. That was the plan. "Call her," Denzil had said. I still couldn't tell from his voice if he'd been serious. Sometimes he said things just because he was bored, to see what would happen. I think he was bored quite a lot. But I'd called her, like I said.

"What's she like?" he'd asked later.

"Oh, she's OK. A bit shy."

"What does she *look* like?"

"OK," I'd said again, and crossed my fingers.

On the phone, she hadn't sounded any different, from the little that she said. There had been an awkward wait while her mother went to call her, and I heard their voices in the background faintly. "Sarah? It's Jon." "Jon?" "You know, *Jon*." "Oh…" Then there'd been a pause – she wasn't exactly running to the phone, then "Hello?"

I'd known that I'd have to do most of the talking – "How's the family?"

"OK."

"Mine too." It wasn't easy. Did she still do her drawing? I asked casually and yes, she said, she did. She wanted to get into art college. She'd relaxed a bit and we were talking, so I slipped it in. "We've got lots to talk about. We could meet for a coffee." Pause. "I've got a friend," I said. "He's into Art." It was a risk. I hadn't asked her if she had a boyfriend, or anything like that. But I could hear she hadn't from the way she said "OK."

I slipped out of the car park and into the road. At the back of the station the viaduct merged into the brick embankment people called The Arches. They'd cleaned up the station approach, but no one came round the back except beat-up vans for the lock-up workshops that had squeezed themselves beneath the arches, walling themselves in with corrugated iron that rattled when a train passed overhead. Inside, I got a glimpse of oily darkness, with sometimes the whine of a drill or a lathe, or the blue tooth of an oxy-acetylene flame and then a plume of orange sparks. *Panel Beating*, one sign said, *Body Work Done While You Wait*. Others looked deserted; on the one with the rusty green sign saying *Pettifer, House Clearance. Jumble Sales. Everything Taken* the only thing not clogged with dust and cobwebs was the padlock and chain on the door.

The last arch, the lowest one, was empty, unless you count crumpled cans and chip wraps. There was a smell that made me walk by quickly and not want to look.

He was there on the pavement in front of me. He hadn't stepped out; he must have been standing there, motionless, arms dangling in his too-small jacket with big hands and half his forearm poking out. His tie, a horrible 1960s Paisley thing today, dangled half undone. He lifted his big round face slowly and his eyes were a too-pale, nearly colourless blue. "Excuse me," he said. "Spare a copper for a cup of tea?"

There was a story about VI, that he had no sense

of taste. Some kids were passing through the station one day and he stopped them with the cup-of-tea line. "OK," said one and he went to the buffet, picked up a cold one someone had left on the table. VI took it, grinned and said "Thank you, sir. Nice." Next time, they picked up a half-drunk polystyrene cup with a fag end in it, topped it up with salt and sugar and gave it a stir. When VI took it they watched, ready to explode with giggling and run away, but he downed it in one go and smiled: "Thank you. Nice." It might have been Denzil who told me. It might have been Denzil who did it, come to that.

"Excuse me." This time VI wouldn't be ignored. For once, he looked me straight in the eye. "Have you seen Auntie? She's gone."

"Sorry," I said feebly and went to walk past him, but he stepped into my way.

"Auntie," he said. "You know."

"I don't know your auntie." For the first time I noticed quite how big he could be, when he wasn't shambling with his head down.

"Excuse me," he said again. "You know her. You were there. She was in the facetaker." And all at once I realized: he meant Alice.

"They took her to hospital. I'm sorry."

"No," he said, with his pale eyes still fixed on me. They never seemed to blink. "She was gone before. In the facetaker. Snap."

* * *

36

When I got to the buffet, Denzil was already waiting, perched on a round stool by the window. He had that impatient look this morning; whatever happened next, it had better be good.

"What kept you?"

I swivelled a stool and sat down by him. Outside the window, crowds were milling to and fro.

"Facetaker…" I said.

"You what?"

"Facetaker. How's that for a new name for a photo booth?"

"Not bad. If you're seven years old. Where's this cousin of yours?"

We both stared through the crowd. You know how printed words can go, when you gaze at a page too hard and suddenly they don't mean anything, just black squiggles on white. That's how it was out there – a thousand empty faces. On the Departures board above them, a list of destinations flickered and folded up – a train must have left – like a pack of cards shuffled up for a new deal. It had always been a little thrill, that moment. It was like being in an airport. I tried to imagine it saying Paris, Singapore, Los Angeles…

All the destinations flickered one space to the left. And then the buffet door swung open. "Jon?" said Sarah's voice, and I knew why I had missed her. There were two of them. "Jon," said Sarah, "this is my friend Claire."

Claire stared at me, sullen, and my heart sank. She didn't want to be there. She had a pinched-up, cross little face, under a thatch of rather savagely chopped dark hair. She didn't want to be stared at, either. Denzil hadn't said a word; he just swivelled his stool and looked them up and down. I knew what he was thinking. I wished he would speak.

"OK" is one of those words that can mean anything, depending how you say it. People use it of me, like: *Jon? Oh, he's OK. Nice bloke. Nothing special.* I'd told Denzil Sarah was OK, and she was, except it meant: Nothing wrong with her. Nothing much to say about her at all. Girls change fast; I've seen my friends' sisters go from being kids to being … well, something special, in the space of a long summer holiday. I'd been hoping that she'd be like that, but she wasn't. She was taller, a little bit more solid, that's all. Her face was nice enough but sort of blank, as if she'd learned from experience that smiling didn't do much good.

"I'm Denzil," Denzil said, and put out a hand to shake. He was polite, brisk, routine. He didn't seem to look at them at all. "I'll get drinks. What do you want?" They both named soft drinks. "Jon? Cappuccino? Latte? Double espresso?" he said. "Come and give me a hand."

At the counter he didn't turn to me. They were bound to be watching us. "What a couple of dogs," he said from the side of his mouth. He slapped a handful of coins on the counter and left the woman counting it. "Ten minutes max. If nothing special happens, I'm off."

"Hold on," I said, slopping the coffees. "You're the one who told me to…" But he was back at the table already, delivering the girls their Fantas with a flourish. He sat himself down as if being their escort was the job he wanted most in all the world.

"Jon tells me you're an artist…" he said. Sarah nodded, tightly. "I'm into the Surrealists," he pressed on. "Do you like Salvador Dali?"

"Not much."

"I wish I could paint my dreams," he said. "Especially the really strange ones. Don't you?"

"I'm doing a project on the Impressionists." There was an awkward pause. Claire just watched. I couldn't tell whether that was a cross look on her face, or whether her forehead and her lips just naturally screwed up that way.

"Yes, dreams…" said Denzil as if she'd agreed with him. "I'm interested in them. It must be the Romany blood. My Hungarian grandmother—"

"What?" I couldn't help myself. I'd heard several of his stories about his family, and all of them were different. This was the fourth or fifth grandmother, at the very least.

"You see?" he said. "There are things about me even my best friends don't know…" And he gave me a look that must have been the same he gave

Lisa in the class with Mr Pinkus. It said: *This is a performance. Don't ask awkward questions. Sit back and enjoy.* Sometimes I couldn't keep up with Denzil. Five minutes earlier he'd been ready to walk out. Now, click: he'd decided that this could be rather entertaining after all.

"She never actually *taught* me about telling fortunes," he said, "but..."

Claire's nose wrinkled up tighter. "You mean crystal balls?" she said. Sarah gave her a look – *Don't mock*, it said, *listen*. Denzil leaned closer to Sarah. "Palms. And cards, of course," he said, to her, not Claire.

"That's rubbish," Claire said.

"Oh?" said Denzil. "Let me show you. Give me your hand." Claire flinched. He turned to Sarah and she gave hers meekly. He took it gently, turned it palm up and she blushed. With a light touch of his index finger he began to trace the lines.

Then he was talking, quickly, lightly, and I don't remember half of it. It was like a bubbling stream of words: "I see people round you ... close ... your family, maybe ... yes, lots of them ... too many, sometimes... I can see you upstairs on your own... I see books..." Most of the words flowed past but now and then something rose to the surface: Sarah nodded, or a shadow crossed her eyes, or she blinked. Denzil was glancing at her palm one moment, then up at her face and talking, talking.

He could see her career ahead. Success, her pictures hung on walls, and travel…

"I can see what you're doing," said Claire sharply. So could I, but I wished she wouldn't spoil it. It was a good performance. He would rattle on, and whenever he touched on something that happened to be true, her eyes or the skin of her hand would say *Yes!*

"Sarah's giving you all the answers," said Claire. "Most of what you're telling her is rubbish."

"Stop it, Claire!" It was the first time I'd heard Sarah raise her voice in anger, ever.

Denzil let go of her hand, and graced them both with a slow smile. "I never said it was magic," he said. "But if you're interested, I can tell you something really strange." He paused. Would Claire dare to say no? "See that photo booth out there?"

And so he told the story. By the time he'd got to the snapshots, when he slipped them out of his pocket even more deftly than he'd done with me, I was watching the girls, willing Claire not to sneer. She didn't. As he laid the photos on the table, she squinted at them, close, then she looked up at Denzil, then she looked at me.

"It's true," I said. "I was there."

"Wow," breathed Sarah, eyes on Denzil.

"Dead," said Claire. "She was really dead?"

I nodded.

"Wish I'd been there."

"Claire!" said Sarah. "That's dreadful." Denzil smiled slightly. He liked a challenge, Denzil. Claire had been a challenge. And he'd won. From that moment Claire was with us, for better or worse.

"What was that you called it?" said Denzil. "The facetaker?"

"It wasn't my idea…" I started.

"No," said Claire. "You're right. Think of those tribes who say that cameras steal your soul." She took a final swig of Fanta. "Perhaps it's true."

"Don't say a word of this to anyone," said Denzil. "Promise?" We all nodded. At a casual glance we might have looked like four kids chatting round a plastic buffet table, but we were a club now, a secret society.

5

First Blood

It was nearly midnight, and the house was quiet for once. No sound of Kate's stereo, with this week's throwaway chart songs. No witter of Keir's kiddie cartoons. No sound of Keir waking up in the night, as he still did, with Mum stumbling in there, grumbling. None of Dad's squeaky twiddly jazz he went away and played to himself in the study when things got too much. No, Mum and Dad were out; he'd booked them a meal for some little anniversary of theirs, a bit embarrassing but sweet, really. So it was a quiet moment. Then the phone rang. I snatched it up quickly, before it woke Keir.

It was Sarah. "Hi," I said. "What are you doing up so late?"

"Oh, nothing," she said, too lightly. "I've just been out with Denzil."

"Out with him? We only saw you at teatime." She and Claire had left together; they hadn't said anything... "You and Claire met him later? I thought we were meant to be a club, all four of us."

"Not Claire. Just me... He just wanted to talk about the art – pictures and portraits, you know – and he couldn't do it so easily when Claire was there. I mean, she's OK, but..."

"I thought she was your friend."

"She is... Oh, men don't understand. No, the thing is, Denzil and I got talking – he's very easy to talk to, isn't he? – and he was saying how the pictures from that booth might have a sort of special something now ... after Alice, I mean. Then I had this idea."

She paused, and the quiet of the house was deeper. Somewhere way off down the hill, I heard the rattle of a late night train. "Remember that silly game," she said, "that Christmas, with the faces? Aunt Bea? Well, the things that Denzil was saying set me thinking: maybe it wasn't so silly. I mean, when I saw you at the station I had a shock. You looked the way I sort of knew you would when you were older. Jon, maybe I really can, you know, sense things, see the future... Denzil thinks so. Then I thought: what if I used photos from that photo booth? I mean, there's something strange about them, isn't there?"

"Sarah?" I said slowly. "Whose idea was this?"

"Mine, of course, Denzil seemed quite surprised, but when he thought about it... Well, he said yes. He said if I wanted to try it out I could do it with photos of him."

For a moment I wanted to tell her how he'd done it, starting with the things I'd told him and leading her on. I should have, but would she have listened? "Oh? Why him?" I said.

"I'll do you next, I promise. He said he'd go first, just in case."

"In case? In case of what?"

"Oh ... nothing. Just, if there's something really strange about that booth, you know. Think of the old woman." I don't know how I sounded to her — not very convinced, I guess — but suddenly she was irritated. "Well, I think he's brave," she said, and there was no mistaking the tone in her voice. Hero worship. "Look, he wants us all to meet tomorrow. Station buffet, eight o'clock. OK?" she said, and put the phone down. It was so sudden I thought she'd been cut off, and waited on the stairs for it to ring again. I waited, then after five minutes went slowly up to the attic.

My room's only got one narrow window, but you can look down from it right across the town. You can see the station, with its lights on even in the small hours. When a train comes in over the viaduct there are these purplish flashes like sheet lightning

– arc flashes from the electricity. The town's in a valley, and it can seem very small. Mum says it makes it snug but sometimes I want to tear down a hill so that I can see somewhere beyond it. Right then I knew there was a wider, stranger world out there, just beyond the horizon. If I could just see over...

I closed my eyes and saw the Destinations board, the names of all the local stations folding up with a clatter and vanishing, which meant a train had gone.

It was just before eight when I got to the station buffet, and I thought I'd got there first. Then I realized the back at the window belonged to Claire. "Hi," I said, "where are the others?"

"Sarah said she'd meet me here," said Claire. Had Sarah told her about meeting Denzil? I don't know why – just something about the way those two were with each other, best-friends-but ... I guessed she hadn't. "Have you seen Denzil since yesterday?" she said.

I shook my head. Now the exams were over people were disappearing fast, getting summer jobs, the kind that numb your brain all day but earn you the money to go out at night. If your parents will let you. I was learning how to punch a till at KwikSave and to say Thank You For Shopping With Us, looking up with a smile for sad old blokes and end-of-tether mums with whinging kids. All day they nudged past – faces, faces…

Claire looked out of the clump of her hair like a sharp-snouted animal sniffing. "How come you're friends with Denzil?"

"Don't know. We just are."

"You seem different, that's all."

"Different? Different from what?"

"From each other. You're so nice and normal, and he's … well, different. Why are you looking like that?"

"Sorry," I said. "It's that *nice and normal*…"

"Some people would give anything to be nice and normal." How many times had I heard it? *Jon? Oh, he's OK, he's nice, you'll like him.* Why did it make me want to scream?

"Me and Sarah," she said. "People think we're close as that." She crooked her two index fingers together. "But it's like we were the only ones left over when everyone else picked their teams…" She froze. I followed her look, behind my shoulder, through the window, and saw what she'd seen. Sarah was coming towards us through the crowd, with Denzil. They were laughing privately.

"Hello," they said together.

"Hi," I said. Claire did not speak.

"*Voilà!*" said Denzil. With a conjuror's flourish he wiped the white plastic table-top, sending sugar wrappers and plastic stirrers on to the floor. Then he laid out eight little rectangles of card, face down, in lines of four. He waited, looking from Claire to me and back again.

"I'm here to report," he said, in a hammed-up mad-scientist voice, "that the experiment was a success. Well, don't you want to see?"

Claire shrugged, "What's all this, then?" and reached for the photos. "No!" Denzil steered her hand away. "Patience. You've got to see them in the right order. Are you ready? Right…"

Click, click, click, click – he flipped over the first row of four. Four Denzil faces, and at first glance there was not much to tell between them. In the first he was just as he was, though a bit pale, the way cheap passport photos make your face look bleached and flat. The second had been touched up slightly round the edges. I could see where Sarah's pen had narrowed the cheeks a little and hardened the jawline – aged him somewhere in his early twenties, like the student-aged older brothers some of my friends had.

In the third he was forty-something, like most of our dads – some lines, a bit of stubble, a receding hairline. In the fourth most of the hair had gone and the cheeks had fallen in; he was old, but still clearly Denzil. She'd done much the same trick as she'd done with me, that Christmas, but with Denzil it didn't seem to make that much difference. With mine, I'd had this shock: is *that* the future?

With him, well, wasn't his face always older than it seemed?

Was this the magic gift he'd been talking her into thinking she had? So what? was all I could think. After all this build-up. I was disappointed.

He was watching me, letting the impression sink in. I hoped he wasn't going to make me say something, in front of Sarah. "Tame," he said, "aren't they? Don't worry, that's what both of us felt. But now, who are these guys?" With four clicks he flipped the next row over.

Four Denzils again. Or they were and they weren't. The first was a lad, a wide-boy with a crimp of wavy hair and a glint in his eyes. Sarah hadn't altered much – I could hardly spot the pen strokes – but the face in the photo was a charmer, a conman, the kind of bloke you wouldn't trust your girlfriend within a mile of. I glanced up at Denzil, just to check.

The second face was a shocker. I didn't know how he could sit there, cool as an ice cube, and let us look at it. The face was a powder-white mask; the eyes were half-shut slits, veiled by long lashes tarred with mascara; the mouth was daubed with blood-red glossy lipstick. Rocky Horror Show, I thought. This was Denzil in drag.

The third had a tangle of beard, thatch eyebrows overhanging wild deep piercing eyes – an Ancient Mariner, a Merlin or Rasputin, some kind of sorcerer. Like old Russian icons' eyes, once those eyes had looked at you they seemed to follow you however you tried to get out of their way. And the fourth? Remember the films I mentioned, with the Mafia boss, Mr Big? That was him, and it was James Bond, and it was the smooth pale Count with the East European accent, who has known all the beautiful women from all the spas of Europe, going back for longer than anyone's memory could possibly go.

"Weird..." breathed Claire. I said, "Sarah, that's brilliant."

She blushed a little. "It just happened," she said.

"Four cards," Denzil said. "Same suit. Nobody told her to do it. See? The Jack, Queen, King and Ace of Guys!" He swept up the first four deftly. "Different, aren't they? Ask Sarah."

"The first ones," she said, "that's all I could do, however hard I tried." She glanced at Denzil. Yes, I could see she had tried really hard, to please him. "But they just felt dull," she said. "An old game. Then he gave me the others ... and I couldn't help it. These other faces ... they were just there, staring out of them. They were sort of alive."

I looked at her face. She was serious. Sarah doesn't get light-hearted very often, but when she gets *really* serious, you can tell.

"Do you want to know what it is, the thing that makes the difference?" said Denzil. He looked at

Claire, daring her to answer. Claire nodded. "Well," he said, "after the first set, let's be honest, I was disappointed. I'd thought there was something about that booth, something paranormal. But it didn't happen." He paused.

"Than I thought: Alice... What was it about her, that one time?"

"She was dead," said Claire. "That's all. A minor difference."

"Yes." He ignored the sarcasm. "She died. I wasn't going to volunteer to be dead, no thanks – not even for the sake of Sarah's art. But I reckoned I could spare a drop of blood. Just a pinprick, from my finger, on the screen. And look what happened..." He spread his palms wide: QED.

"For it to work..." he said. "Don't ask me what *it* is, but you can see it, can't you? This isn't just Sarah doing pictures – all due respect to Sarah – this stuff comes from *somewhere else*. Well, for it to work..." He paused. "It seems to need some kind of sacrifice."

6

Guys and Dolls

I steered through the crowd to where the photo booth was waiting. The Facetaker. People steered into my path as if they were trying to slow me down – to give me time to think. Me, I just wished the crowd was denser, so the others couldn't see me from the buffet window ... but I could feel their gaze between my shoulder blades all the time.

"Let me come and watch you do it," said Claire. "Go on, please…" For the first time she blinked her eyes wide open – greyish-green, and slightly bulging – and fixed them on me.

"No." I squirmed and knew that I was blushing. "Private."

"How will we know you've really done it?" she said. "With the blood and everything."

"Trust Sarah," said Denzil quietly. "She'll know."

The booth was empty. I slipped in and pulled the curtain. Was there still the faintest smell in here? I wondered if anyone had come and disinfected it. Had there been blood when Alice died, or worse? I tried not to think of it, right now. I spun the red plastic seat to wind it lower. It rattled down, bolted with four chunky bolts to the floor.

The blood. All I had to do was prick my finger, but what with? I hadn't thought. There was nothing in my pockets, unless you counted a key or a biro. Shamefaced, I stepped out into the crowd again.

In the entrance of the station, people ran the gauntlet. On one side there'd be a beggar with his bit of cardboard, on the other, a charity collector with an official badge and a rattly tin. Sometimes they stared at each other so fiercely you could hardly walk between them. Today we had a heart foundation; for the usual stray coin you got a little sticker. For a pound you got a small paper rose, deep crimson … with a tiny safety pin. "*Thank* you, young man," said the woman with the tin and insisted on pinning it on my sweatshirt. I was already undoing it as I walked back to the photo booth.

"Excuse me." I turned round. "That's a pretty flower." It was VI. He'd materialized from nowhere, from out of the crowd, and he was tagging along with me. "Excuse me," he said. I speeded up. "Pretty," he said, quickening his pace too, grinning doggily. "Can I have one, for my brother?"

"Here!" I said, thrusting the paper flower at him. He took it in both hands and gazed at it, wondering. Then he frowned.

"No pin," he said.

"No pin. Just hold it." And I ducked inside the kiosk. If you could slam a curtain, I'd have slammed it then. I sat on the stool with the safety pin open. Ready…

Through the small dark pane of glass in front of me a green bulb glowed. By its light you could see a matt black inner chamber, like a spooky doll's house or the tank in the nocturnal building at the zoo, one that always looks empty till you realize there's a little spider in the corner, as dull as a piece of crumpled paper and as deadly as a loaded gun.

Eye Level, said a sign on either side. As I adjusted myself, my face appeared, almost in silhouette, a dark ghost. I could see the slight glint of my eyes.

The pin…

Then I noticed the humming, or halfway between a hum and a mumble, with a rhythm like a playground chant. It should have been a child's voice, but it wasn't. VI was stood outside the booth, quite close outside. It was putting me off. The pin wavered. Just ignore him Jon, I thought. He'll get bored and go away. But next time it was louder.

"Go away!" I poked my head out through the curtain, to face him. But he'd melted back into the crowd, as he'd appeared to come out of it. However slow he seemed, VI could move quickly when he wanted to.

The pin…

Which finger did they use in blood donation? I squeezed my left thumb, and touched it with the pin tip.

What if the booth hadn't been disinfected? What if my hands had touched the seat, where she…?

Back in the buffet, Sarah, Claire and Denzil would be getting restless. In a moment they would come and look. The station announcer's voice came, crackly, sing-song: *We apologize for the delay to the eight-fifteen from London. This is due to an incident on the line.* I gave a little stab. It hurt, but didn't break the skin. Again. I squeezed. Yes, just a tiny drop of blood.

I fed the coins in the slot – two pounds, a fifty – and waited. Clunk. One of the pounds clattered down into the Return slot. I licked it and pushed it back in. A click, like pinball, and the green light in the screen went red. Now. What should I do with the blood? I dabbed the single drop of it between the eyes of my reflection, like an Indian caste mark, and sat upright, my eyes on the line.

There was a pause, like firing squad victims must register, only they never get to tell you, do they? Flash. As I blinked, a green after-image shivered behind my eyes, then there was the red light again. Should I smile? Flash.

Before the third flash I thought: what if that's where Denzil dabbed his blood, in the very same spot? Flash. Did that make us blood brothers? Flash, it went again.

Sarah didn't call the next day, or the next. Every time the doorbell rang, or the phone went, I would jump. Kate raised her eyebrows, as if to say *Well? Who is she?*

I phoned Denzil.

"Give her time," he said. "She's an artist. This is a major work. You'll see."

On the third day, the doorbell went. Kate got there first, and was halfway up the stairs as I came down. "Sarah!" she muttered. "Well, well…" and she started humming one of her irritating chart songs. *Baby baby you're the only one for me…*

"Sorry," said Sarah, on the doorstep. "Mum's starting to notice I'm going out a lot. She'll ask questions."

"So?"

Sarah lowered her eyes. "I'd just rather she didn't, that's all. You haven't told anyone, have you?"

"No. Why should I?" I wanted to say: *But it's only a game.* There was something in her eyes that stopped me.

"That's OK. I don't know what Denzil would do if you did." She was whispering now. Just as well: I caught the slight creak that said Kate was on the landing. "You know Denzil," said Sarah. It wasn't a question, but it should have been.

"I'd better warn you," she said up in my room; we'd closed the door behind us. "Some of them have come out a bit strange. Don't worry; you can see mine too." She started to deal the cards out, one by one.

She'd been working. Far from just passport photos, they were proper playing cards now, with the snapshots pasted in the middle and an ornamental border round them. She'd even dog-eared them a bit and treated them – cold tea, she told me later – to make them look old. She laid them out in suits. The four we'd seen before, of Denzil: Ace, King, Queen and Jack of Guys. Then the four of herself, in several kinds of make-up, like she never wore. One was dead glamorous, with big hair and fluttering eyelids; one was cute and round-cheeked, baby-pretty with her hair in bunches; one slant-eyed and fierce; one an aristocrat, with a little tiara and fur stole. Somewhere back as a kid, she must have had too many Barbies and Spice Girls. She'd put right her slightly wonky teeth and made them just too white, too perfect. All four versions looked mask-like, plastic and a little scary. No, it wasn't Sarah, just as Denzil's four weren't him ... except maybe they *were* parts of them, the secret parts you don't see.

So that was it. A suit each. If Denzil's suit was Guys, then these were Dolls. And me? What would I be?

"You've got to see Claire's," Sarah said, and dealt them. Whatever she'd done to her own, she'd done the opposite to Claire's face. Whatever detail was slightly out of true – a spot on the chin, the lopsided slant of the nose – she had exaggerated. One was a vampire, with her whitened face, thin black lips, the tip of a fang. One was an imp, an evil sprite with a grin too wide by half. There was a loopy-eyed sorceress, a Queen of the Night; there was one with an unnerving slanty smile and horribly long fingers.

If Claire saw these, she'd go mad.

"I couldn't help it," said Sarah. "That's how they came out. We call them the Ghouls."

"And mine?" I said.

Sarah dealt the first one and looked up, her hand still shielding it. "You've got to understand," she said. "This isn't *you*." Two, three, four. I stared. They stared back – wall-eyed, hunchbacked, snaggle-toothed, bald and crazy.

"What do you call them?" I said.

"The Weirds. Jon? Say something."

"It's only a game," I said as she gathered them in. "What now? Is that it?"

"No, no. Denzil's going to read them. Remember what he said about his gypsy grandma…"

"Sarah," I said carefully. "Denzil's very good at … at making up stories." She shot me a sharp look. I couldn't go on.

"Maybe," she said, "you don't know him as well as you think you do." She was brisk now, and not looking at me. "I'd better get home."

"Kate will be disappointed. She thinks you're here for a date."

Sarah flushed. On the doorstep, she stopped and looked at me. "Jon," she said. "There's only one thing I'm worried about. It's Claire. She's had … emotional problems in the past, you know."

"I don't know anything about her. She's your friend."

"I'm not sure about *friend*. We just got put together at school, for some reason. I'm just thinking of her. It might be better if she didn't get … too involved, you know?"

"Sarah, what are you saying?"

"Claire can get very … attached to people. Too much. Better for people not to encourage her…" A car door slammed in the street. It was Dad coming home. Sarah bit her lip.

"What do you mean?" I said.

She shook her head. "See you," she muttered, and was gone.

"That was quick," said Kate on the landing.

"Were you listening?" I said. "If you were, I'll…"

"Keep your hair on." I wished I had the card of me – the King, I think it was – with the shaved head and the eyepatch and the pipe in the shape of a small skull clamped between his broken teeth. He'd sort out my silly kid sister, if I couldn't handle it myself.

Upstairs, an hour later, in bed, I found I was thinking of Claire. It wasn't fair, what Sarah had done to her pictures … even if she claimed it wasn't really *her*. She wasn't that bad looking. From some angles, she was kind of appealing in a funny-faced way. At least when she smiled. She hadn't smiled often yet, but when she had, it seemed to be at me more than the others. I found myself remembering how she leaned quite close that day and said, "You've got to let me watch." Was that when Sarah had first noticed her fancying me? Had Claire talked about it later? If not, how did Sarah know? And what right had she got to say *Don't encourage her?* I felt suddenly sorry for Claire, the way Sarah was going off with Denzil. Maybe I should talk to her, just to make sure she was all right?

I tiptoed downstairs and took the phone into the

cupboard under the stairs. I rang Sarah. It was engaged. I stayed there hunched under the stairs, taking deep breaths, then dialled again.

"Hi, Sarah," I said, as lightly as I could. "I meant to ask you earlier... Have you got Claire's phone number there by any chance?"

"Jon," said Sarah, "I'd leave it. I think you should let her sort out the Denzil thing by herself."

"What do you mean, the Denzil thing?"

"She fancies him, of course!" Sarah swallowed the last word. "Oh, God, Jon, you didn't think I meant you, did you?"

"No, of course not. Don't be stupid." I might have put the phone down rather hard, because a moment later there was a well-known squeaking noise from upstairs. It was Keir starting up for a cry. By the time I reached the landing there was Mum already. "Now look what you've done," she hissed. "Creeping downstairs. Making noise. He'll have us awake for an hour now."

"Sorry."

"I should think so. Who were you phoning at this time?"

"Just a friend." I knew it sounded shifty. But we're meant to, aren't we, teenagers? I thought that was normal.

"Honestly, Jon," she said. "This isn't like you at all. I don't know what's got into you." Just then Keir changed up into top gear, wailing. Kate looked out of her doorway, as if she happened to be just on her way to the bathroom. "Night night," she said knowingly.

"Sleep well," I said. For a moment I enjoyed the thought of what the King of Weirds could do to my kid sister in her dreams.

7

Jack of Ghouls

It was nearly the end of my shift at KwikSave and I was punch drunk with it. Everything was passing in a blur. The next trolley rattled up and I waited for the avalanche of dog food and washing powder to begin. It didn't. Come to think of it, the trolley had clattered oddly, as if it was empty. I looked up and there was Denzil. "Hi," he said. "Like the photos?"

"Can't talk now," I muttered. "Manager's watching." There wasn't a queue behind him yet, but there would be. "I'm off in ten minutes. Just wait a tick." I should have remembered: Denzil never waited. Denzil never queued.

"I thought you were *meant* to be friendly," he said. "You know: Thank You For Shopping With Us?"

"You aren't shopping."

"Yes, I am." He reached into his trolley and brought out the packet of crisps. Quite an expensive brand, it's true, but still, one packet. Behind him trolleys were arriving. "You don't want to serve these people, really..." Denzil said.

"Are you buying that or aren't you?"

He grinned. "Wait a moment," he said, loudly. "This roast-beef-and-horseradish flavour... Is that British beef? Does it have BSE?"

"I don't know. Look on the packet."

Denzil held it up, so the five shoppers and three kids behind him could see and hear. "It doesn't say."

"Change it!" I said, through gritted teeth.

"OK... Sorry..." Now he was pushing the empty trolley back through the checkout, squeezing past the loaded trolleys, piling up the queue. He gave each angry face a winning little smile.

"Wake up!" said a woman's voice. She had unloaded a week's worth of pizzas on the belt and I hadn't even noticed. I'd been looking at the people's faces, vacant and impatient. In my mind I'd been felt-penning in the details – horns and teeth for the grown-ups, and the little kids had snouts and whiskers. "Wake up, young man. I haven't got all day."

Denzil was right. I didn't want to serve these people. I wanted to upend their trolleys and listen

64

to the smash of breaking glass, and laugh and laugh. The Jack of Weirds would do it, even if I'd never dare.

And there was the store manager, coming over. I beeped the pizzas through the barcode reader. "Thank you for shopping with us, madam," I said, and smiled.

In the staff washroom I peered in the mirror and tried to remember how the cards looked. Jack, Queen, King and Ace of Weirds... I tried narrowing my eyes to lizard slits, I tried rolling my lips back to show all my teeth. With an effort I could hold a scowl or a creepy stare for ten seconds or so, then I'd laugh, and there was my own face again. Nice normal Jon. It was a pleasant sort of face, nothing wrong with it at all. I gave it one more scowl, then hurried out to see if Denzil had bothered to wait, or if he'd found something more special to do.

"What's all this gypsy business?" I said. He was there on the pavement. "You're making it up, aren't you?"

He shrugged. It always annoyed me when he did that, especially now.

"That business back in the shop. You could really get me into trouble. As it was, the manager asked if I knew you. He didn't really believe me when I said no."

We came into the station concourse, into the familiar smell of diesel, coffee, soot and people's sweat.

"You should tell him where to put his lousy job," he said. "It's slave wages, anyway."

"It's all right for you!"

"How do you know?" he said sharply, then looked up and waved. "Look, there are the girls…" For a moment we could have been two normal people on a normal double-date.

"Anyway," he said as we crossed the space towards them, "my grandmother was Hungarian. Lots of Hungarians have gypsy blood."

It was our usual table by the window. Over in the corner an electronic fruit machine was flashing Wheel Of Fortune, flickering spangles of red, yellow and gold light, with pound signs in them. They glinted on the sweaty bald patch of a man who pushed his coins in, punched the buttons, sighed and kicked the machine, then stumped back to the bar.

"We've all seen the cards," said Denzil. "Brilliant, Sarah." Like a conjuror's assistant she produced them, holding them out for him to take. He did, without looking, gave them a quick snappy shuffle and put the pile precisely, face down, in the middle of the table.

"Who wants to go first?" he said. "I'll keep it simple. It's not like the whole Tarot pack. Well…?"

There was a hollow rattle. The bald man was back at the fruit machine, winning a little. You win just enough to keep you playing. That's how it works. Otherwise, who'd be a sucker?

"Claire?" said Denzil.

"Me? Why me?"

"Because you want to," he said quietly. "You know you do."

She looked up and met his eyes, and neither of them blinked. "OK," she said. "What do I have to do?"

"Just pass your hand across the cards," he said and launched into the patter, in a quick light sing-song voice, with just the hint of an Eastern European accent. "Let them sense you. Now, rest your hand on them a moment. Don't think. Don't speak. Whatever's in your secret mind, they'll know." It could have been funny – Denzil improvising as a fairground Tarot reader – but there was something in the air. That power of his. As Claire's hand touched the cards he laid his on it, lightly, pressing it down on the cards. "Now…" he went on with hardly a pause. "I shuffle and I spread the cards … like this…"

With a sweep of the hand, he sketched a circle in the air. "East, North, West, South," he muttered. "An eye, an eye, a nose, a mouth…" He laid four cards, still face down, on the table. Two were end to end, not touching. The third was between them, lower and at right angles. Below it, the fourth was parallel with the first two. "Quickly ... what do you see?" said Denzil.

"A face. Two eyes, a nose, a mouth," said Claire.

"Exactly. The Face of Fate. Look at it hard and don't blink. Let your eyes go out of focus. The Face. Your face. Now it's looking at you, looking deep inside you, deeper, deeper..."

"Claire," said Sarah, "you don't have to. Denzil..."

Claire didn't look up; she was locked on the cards, and Denzil didn't take his eyes off her.

"Good," he said. "Now let's see if the Face will tell me what it sees." With a pass of his hand he sketched the circle again in the air, then with two quick flicks: "An eye. An eye. The King of Weirds. Who is he? Someone close to you. Older. But not wiser. And look at his eyes..."

That face: it had started as me, but it had fallen on bad times, really bad. A day-and-a-half of stubble on its chin didn't quite hide the dull bruised look of the cheeks; the eyes were bloodshot, dull and yellowing. Shadows gathered in the deep lines round the eyes, which gazed out at us as if to say *Stop staring. Leave me alone.* "You'll know who it is. Don't say. And there's the Queen of Dolls, laid the opposite way. Hmmm..."

"What does that mean?" Claire was watching him steadily now. He flicked over the card in the centre. "Two eyes, two I's, two people just thinking about themselves... Not facing each other. Two people can't see eye to eye. That leaves one on their own, the nose, you see: the one who knows —" he tapped his own nose in that *I-know-something-you-don't* gesture — "who knows too much. Look, it's the Jack of Ghouls. One of your cards."

"Stop it," Sarah said, and she meant it. Claire was very pale and stretched tight, as if she could snap. Denzil was watching her, too. Any moment now, I thought, she's going to sweep the lot off the table and say *Fooled you. I was leading you on.* But no: he had her, with that power. She was on his hook.

"Stop it," said Sarah again. "It's cruel..."

"Go on," said Claire coldly. I never found out what it was about Claire's family, but it was difficult; I don't know where Denzil was getting it either, but he was laying out something in front of our eyes, something Claire recognized, and couldn't look away from.

"Is this the future?" she said. "Like: how it's got to be?"

"This is the past," he said. "You want to see the future?"

"That's enough of that!" The frosty voice came from behind us, and I turned to see a short woman with tightly-crimped grey hair and an apron. The last time I saw her she had been behind the counter.

"You'll stop right there, thank you. We'll not have any of that in here."

"Excuse *me*," said Denzil. "We were only playing cards. And not for money, if that's what you're worried about."

"You know what I mean," said the woman. "The occult. Truckling with the devil. I might be only a tea lady to you, but I'm a Christian woman and I won't have such things going on in my buffet."

"I'll complain," said Denzil. "I'll write to the Catering Manager."

She stiffened. "As you wish," she said. People were starting to turn and watch. "I'd rather lose my job than—"

"Oh, come on..." I just wanted to laugh. She was short and angry. As she pulled herself upright, her neck bobbed like an angry hen's. "It's only a game," I said.

She pulled herself up tighter and held me in a long sad look, then shook her head. "That's what they always think," she said, "until they find out who they're playing with."

Outside, Denzil gave a little snort of laughter. "Stupid bat," he said. "She'll be in some kind of sect, Jehovah's Witnesses or something. And I hadn't finished my coffee. And more to the point..." He turned to Claire. "We hadn't finished with you."

"Leave it," said Sarah. "I don't think you should. If Claire doesn't want..."

Claire spun round at her. "If Claire doesn't *what*? Claire can speak for herself, thank you. I've got the cards," she said to Denzil. "Where can we go?"

"Another cafe?" I said.

"No," said Claire. "Somewhere private. Denzil...?"

He was thinking. "Close to the station, though," he said. "We've got to be close to the booth. I know," he said suddenly. "I've seen a place that should be private."

As soon as we left the station entrance and turned left I guessed where we were going. Behind where the taxis pulled in and their drivers leaned on their bonnets or sat in their cabs, their newspapers spread on the steering wheel, a small road led down and bent round beneath the station. It led down to the long brick wall, the archways, where I'd been before.

There was the first low opening, the empty one, with the smell and the litter.

"There," said Denzil. "That's empty."

"We can't go in there." Sarah was peering into the shadows and I saw what she saw: bundled up grey blankets, like a crumpled nest. So this was where they came from, Alice and the others. "It's someone's place," she said.

"No one's there now."

"It doesn't feel right."

"I want a look," said Denzil, in that way he did

when something caught his interest – not what he'd planned maybe, but suddenly he'd think: *Yes! Why not?* and go for it. Like I said, he was an improviser; he never did like being tied down to a script.

By the time I'd taken a deep breath and caught up with him he was deep inside. It felt like a tunnel, stretching back into the dark, and the builders must have used it for their rubble, the way it sloped up towards the back. He was looking down at a patch of ashes and charred knuckle-shapes of wood: a fire-pit. I thought of caves I'd seen, with evidence of Stone Age occupation. I looked at the bricks above, blackened with smoke, and imagined paintings daubed in ochre mud and red like blood and black of soot. A Stone Age cave, though, would not have had the cider bottles, green or brown, that glinted at our feet.

"Hey, look…" Now my eyes were used to it, they made out shapes on the floor – soggy layers of cardboard where someone had folded big packing cases flat, newspapers and another set of blankets. "Imagine," said Denzil in a low voice. "You could sleep here overnight. Pretend you're homeless. Just feel what it's like."

"Yuck…" said Sarah, in a little-girl voice that annoyed me. I knew what he meant. Haven't you ever lain in bed and heard a sound outside – maybe a train in the distance, or a dog's bark, or a siren – and wondered what it would be like to be out there?

"Don't you get that feeling," Denzil said, "that you'd like to try, just try, being somebody else?"

"I do," said Claire, in the darkness behind me, but Denzil was ferreting deeper in. "And look at *this*…" I recognized the shopping trolley with its freight of poly-bags. Alice's.

Sarah shuddered. "All those bags. I always wondered what was in them."

"Well, now you can look."

"Denzil, no! That's … that feels wrong."

"Go on. You want to."

Very warily, she put out her hand, the way people touch an electric fence they're almost certain isn't switched on, but…

With a rattle, the trolley jerked back. Sarah yelped as if stung. Denzil grabbed at the trolley and yanked it aside. Crouched on the floor behind it was a dark shape as big as a cave bear. It reared up with a roar. "No," it went, "No!" The girls flinched; so did I, but Denzil stood his ground; I'll give him that.

The shape steadied itself and peered at us, eyes narrowed. Then straightened its tie. "Excuse me," it said in that much-too-childish voice. "These are Auntie's things. Only Auntie's friends can use them. She wouldn't like strangers to have them, no."

8

Auntie's Wardrobe

"Shush," said VI suddenly. "Nearly woke my brother." He made a vague sign up and back into the darkness. My eyes were used to it by now, but I couldn't see anybody. "Lucky," said VI. "He doesn't like surprises. He gets angry, very angry."

"It's OK," I said. "You know us. Remember?"

"Oh yes. I've seen you. I remember everything. I thought you'd come to take Auntie's things."

"We don't want to take anything. We were only looking."

"You want to see Auntie's things," said VI. "They're pretty. Very pretty." We looked at each other, awkward now, but he was already undoing a bundle. He pulled out a handful and shook it and there was a long slim lacy nightie. I could hear

Claire draw a breath, not sure whether to laugh or what. VI plunged his hand in again and pulled out a shawl, a bikini top, a clump of cheap necklaces, a shapeless sweater, high-heeled shoes. And that was only the first bag.

"This was hers?" I said. "Where does it come from?"

"Auntie's Wardrobe," he said proudly, and he pointed somewhere I couldn't make out, back into the dark, to one side and up, the way he'd done when he mentioned his brother.

"Next door," said Claire. "It said House Clearances. You know…" she said in a lower voice, "like when people have died."

VI was nodding. "She couldn't squeeze through," he said. "Too wide, poor Auntie. But I fetched things for her. I could get through the crack. You want to see?"

"Uh… What about your brother?" I said.

"Friends now," he said. "He'll like you. You can meet my brother too."

"This is it," Denzil whispered. "This could be our place."

It had been a squeeze for us, following VI. "No," Sarah had said. "We'll all get filthy…" But Claire was nodding, and if Claire and Denzil were going in, so was Sarah. Me too.

It wasn't a passage, more a kind of duct the

builders had laid pipes through, as an afterthought, from the back of one archway to the other. It was too low for us to do more than crouch in, it dripped dust and water down our necks. Sarah was right, we'd be filthy. It would take some explaining.

Through the little passage was a crack of faint light, then VI pushed through something and held it open and we came out blinking. VI let the heavy oil-cloth curtain fall back, and we looked round at a kind of storeroom piled with things.

Things... I mean everything you can imagine no one wanting at a jumble sale. I'd never thought what happened to the stuff left over, when even the faithful have bought everything they can bring themselves to carry. Of course, there are people who move in with vans, a small business arrangement: *We can take the whole lot off your hands.* Where it would ever end up, I'd no idea, but it was stacked up here for now – years and years of sales and emptied houses. When someone dies and there's no one to sort things out, or the family can't bear to, they get the clearance people in and say: *Just take it away.*

What happens, I wondered, when the clearance people die or go bust? It didn't look as if anyone had been in here for years. In the half-light from cracks in the shuttered-up windows, I could make out packing cases piled with fabrics, and the musty smell of utterly abandoned clothes. Auntie's wardrobe. It explained one thing. VI was standing by a tea chest, utterly absorbed, rummaging through a mass of scarves, cravats and ties. Wherever his brother was, he was still asleep.

"Where's the light in here?" said Denzil. I felt my way around the walls where I could get to them, and found the switch where you'd expect it, by the door. I clicked it. Nothing. If it had ever been connected, it had been cut off long ago.

"Look, there's an upstairs too," said Denzil. There was a sudden square of light as he came to the top of the squat wooden ladder and pushed, hingeing up a kind of trapdoor in the ceiling.

"Don't!" I hissed at him. "The brother…!" But there was a chuckle behind me. VI had fastened his tie and was admiring himself in the light from above, reflected in a dusty full–length mirror. "Here's my brother," he said. "Say hello."

"Hello," I said to the mirror.

"Good," said VI. "Friends now. Make yourself at home."

Up the stairs, through the hatch, I blinked in daylight from a tiny window. We were up in the top of the arch, a space not tall enough to stand up in, even in the centre – more a loft than a room – but beneath the narrow window was a table, furred with dust. The two mugs on it can't have been empty, because the bottom half an inch of each was hairy mould. There was no sign that anyone had been there since that tea break was abandoned, and there was the table, just waiting for us all this time.

There was an old paraffin lamp, with a dirty glass funnel, and a box of matches. Denzil grinned as it bloomed, first blue then a yellowish glow. "Where's Sarah?" he said. "I'll get her up here…" He picked up the lamp and clambered back downstairs, letting the hatch bang behind him, and we waited. In a minute I heard them both laughing.

"What are they doing now?" said Claire. She laid the cards down on the table, in a neat pile, and a little puff of dust rose up. After the glow of the lamp, the light from the window seemed pale and thin. We waited. Every now and then, downstairs, they laughed again.

"He said we were going to get on with the game." Claire's lips were tight now. "We haven't finished…"

"Claire," I said quickly. "Listen. Denzil's my friend, but…"

"But what?"

"I don't know what he was doing with the cards just now, but you know it wasn't magic. You saw what he did when he read Sarah's palm."

"That was different. I wasn't helping him like she was. He was really getting things … you know, about my family. Things he couldn't have known."

"Unless Sarah told him," I said. "You know they've been together…"

Claire was quiet. "She wouldn't tell him things like that. I mean, secrets. Would she?"

"Denzil can be very … persuasive."

"Why are you saying this, Jon? I thought he was your friend."

"He is, but… There was this teacher at school…" And I told her the story about Mr Pinkus. She listened, head bowed. I tried hard not to make it sound funny, but she smiled a little. "It was cruel," I said. "We all were. But it was Denzil's idea."

"Why are you saying this?" She bit her lip. "Why are you blaming everything on him, when … when … I know," she said suddenly. "I know why. You're jealous!"

"What?" It was good it was dark. I could feel my cheeks flush.

"Yes," she said. "It's Sarah, isn't it?" Then there was thunder, a gathering rumble that drowned out my *No!* As the train went overhead the brickwork shuddered, the pane rattled in the little window and a fine spray of dust and grit rained down around us. Then, on cue, the trapdoor opened and two figures climbed into the room.

The one behind was Denzil, the one in front a life-size Queen of Dolls. The tasteful crescent of tiara on her forehead must have been glass, not real diamonds, but the fur stole was no imitation. A tattered fox, it glared from orange eyes, its jaws clamped on its tail. As for the girl … it might have been the way she came up the ladder, or just the gear, but there was something in her manner – haughty, poised, commanding – that was not like anyone I knew … for the blink of an eye. Then she turned, a bit too fast, and the tiara slipped. Denzil reached to catch it and she blushed, and it was Sarah after all.

"Kids." Claire was looking at them, motionless and icy. "Kids dressing up." She swept up the cards. "I'm going home."

"Hold on," said Denzil, "the cards…"

She pushed past. "Don't bother. Finish your fancy dress party. Jon was right: it was only a game."

"Claire?" I called after her.

Her face appeared in the hatchway, her eyes pink with held-in tears. "Don't worry about me. If you want a fourth, you can ask VI, can't you?" Then she was gone. Sarah was standing with the fur and the tiara hanging limply in her hand.

"I'd better go after her," she said. She bit her lip. "Oh, why does she always have to spoil things?" By the time we were out on the road there was no sign of Claire. Sarah hurried up towards the station and did not look back.

"What was all that about?" said Denzil. Before I could think what to say, there was VI beside us. He was smiling again, that wide fixed moony smile that all of a sudden did not look so stupid after all.

"Come back soon," he said, "you and your pretty ladies. My brother likes that. Friends." Then he held out his hand. "Auntie got us things," he said. "Food, presents. Nobody to give us things now. We lost our train fare, you know…" Denzil went to step past him, but VI sidestepped, blocking his path, all without a waver in that fixed smile.

"All right," muttered Denzil and dug in his pocket for some small change. VI stood aside and watched us with the same expression as we walked away.

"Don't you ever stop?" I said. We were sat on the edge of the wall, our feet dangling. Beneath, the river glinted darkly. Dusk had come on while we walked. We weren't going anywhere, but down through the park between the embankment and the river seemed good enough. There was no one around but a few late dog-walkers and a courting couple here and there. We'd walked in silence, fuming inside. At least, I was fuming. Everything had gone sour, and it was his fault. What Denzil was thinking, I couldn't tell.

"Don't you ever stop?"

"What?"

"Play-acting?"

He looked up from the water sharply. "No!" He frowned, as if he really was thinking now. "Nobody does – including you. It's just you only do one part – good old Jon, the nice guy."

Nice … ordinary … normal… Jon? Oh, he's OK.
There were times when Denzil seemed to know what I was thinking. "And what's wrong with that?" I said, stung.

"Did I say it was wrong?" He brushed a stone off the wall and it hit the water with a small splash. "You don't *really* want to be different."

"What if I do?"

He looked at me, faintly amused, but kind of sad too. Pensive. Then he shook his head.

"OK," I said. "If that's what you think…" I heaved my feet back over the wall and stood up. "I'll be going."

"OK," he said.

"And another thing…" I turned back. "I hope you realize what you did to Claire."

"Me?"

"Yes. You really touched on something there. You saw her face…"

"You like her, don't you?"

"No… I mean, that's not the point… Anyway, you're the one she fancies."

Denzil raised his eyebrows slightly. "Actually," he said. "I was going to fix that for you. Next deal of the cards, she was going to get one of yours alongside one of hers, facing…"

"Oh yes. How do you know?"

He grinned. "Come on… I might not be a fortune teller, but I do know how to cheat at cards." So even that had been a game. I turned away.

"I could fix it for you and Claire," he said.

"I didn't say I liked her," I said. "You're welcome. Help yourself."

Twenty paces down the path I looked back. Denzil had not moved. He was staring down into the water, looking rather small. "You can't just sit there," I said. "What about your parents? They'll get mad with you."

"No," he said. "I come in when I want to. If I want I can stay out all night."

"Stay out? Where?"

"Oh, anywhere. Clubs, sometimes. Or just walking. And you needn't look like that. They're cool, my parents. We've got an arrangement, like they've got with each other. They don't interfere. That's great, isn't it? You're dead envious, aren't you?"

"Of course I am," I said.

"Really? Can you imagine it?"

"Can I swap?" I said, thinking of Kate. She was always on my case. Any time I was out five minutes after curfew, even if Mum hadn't noticed, she'd make sure she knew.

"You wouldn't want to. Not really. Like my old school. You'd have liked that, would you?"

"Sure." Everything I'd heard about Darkington – no rules, no uniform, no lessons if you didn't fancy it – sounded great.

"Most years, there'd be somebody ran away or topped themselves. Last year, they found one in the swimming pool." He stared down into the water. "Stay ordinary, Jon. Stay boring."

"Stop," I said. "Who says I'm ordinary...?" For some reason I had this sort of burning feeling rising up behind my eyes.

"Jon," said Denzil, "the thing about you being so damned normal is ... I envy you."

"Huh," I said.

"I mean it."

"Well, then," I said, "you could try *acting* normal. Like: being nice to people for a change."

He shrugged. It was annoying enough, the way he shrugged, at the best of times. Right then, you'd think I'd want to push him off that wall. But he looked sort of hopeless. He stared down into the water, till I came back over and stared down with him.

"You believe in it, don't you?" he said. "The facetaker."

"What? You just said you cheated. Just a silly game."

"No, no. That's just the card trick."

"Why?"

"For the girls. They love it," he grinned, then was suddenly serious again. He could change like that, in a second, like a cloud across the sun. "But the facetaker's real – something about it, don't understand what. It *makes things happen*. And the girls know it too. *They* want to be different, you can see it. Do you think either of them *likes* who they are?" He looked up suddenly, straight at me. "And the facetaker… It's a once-in-a-lifetime chance to do it. Change. You wait and see."

"I don't understand you. A minute ago you were saying: be ordinary. Stay normal."

"It's easier that way," he said. "Or so they tell me. I wouldn't know."

I looked down. There were our reflections, side by side, bending slightly in the ripples. With the orange light of the street lamps behind us, I couldn't make out either of our faces. We were outlines, just an image on the surface of the water as it pulled away beneath us, slow, strong and I didn't know how deep – black water always slipping out of reach, downstream.

9

Stray Cat

The phone rang in the middle of supper. Kate jumped up to get it. "If it's one of those telesales people," Dad said, "give it to me. I'll show them." He's a mild bloke, my dad, but he can be dead sarcastic on the phone. I rather hoped it was one of those people, so we could listen. Most of the time he was so quiet that you felt he'd parked his body with us while his mind was somewhere else, not back from work, maybe – Mum was always on at him about the amount of overtime he did. *You should just say no*, she told him, but he shook his head, and said it wasn't as easy as that.

"Hello?" said Kate. She put her head on one side, with a smirk. "Hold on," she said, "I'll get him. Jon!" she called, as if I was half a mile away. "It's one of your women."

"Sorry…" I began, but Claire cut in. Her voice was hushed but urgent. "Can you meet me?"

"What? When?"

"Now."

"We're in the middle of supper…"

"By the Arches," she said. "Jon, I need…" and it went dead. She must have been in a call box, not at home. I put the receiver down. In a moment it would ring again, and I could say, "Not now. Later." But it didn't.

"Your spaghetti's going cold," said Mum. "It'll be spoiled."

It was. All of a sudden I didn't feel like eating anyway.

"Stupid," Claire said. "Not you – me! A real wimp. I meant to do it on my own." I was still catching my breath. I'd got there in ten minutes flat. She looked more annoyed than grateful. As I'd run, my mind had run on faster: she was asking for me. Just me. Not all of us, not Denzil. Me. He'd said that he could fix it. How could he have done it so soon?

That card house of thoughts collapsed, with one look at her face.

"Wanted to do what on your own?" I said lamely.

She'd stepped out of the cover of a doorway. How long would she have waited if I hadn't come?

She was pale, and shaking slightly. "Are you all right?" I said.

"Fine!" She sounded out of breath, as if she'd been running too. "Never better!" There was a kind of fierceness in her voice I didn't understand.

"To do what on your own?" I said again.

"I just need to get inside," she said. "The Wardrobe... But that weird bloke's in there."

"VI?"

"VI. He gives me the creeps. That stuff about his brother. You'd have thought I could handle him easily after ... after..."

"After what? Claire, what's going on?"

"Let's get inside," she said. "I'll tell you later."

At first I thought he wasn't in there. It wasn't until we were halfway into his brick cave, blinking at the dark, that he rose up in front of us, out of the shadows. He swayed, looking up and down, right and left, behind us.

"One, two," he said. "No friends? Just you?" He gave a flat little giggle.

"We need to go next door," I said. He didn't move. "To look at the clothes," I said, slowly. "Is that OK?"

"Nice." He grinned broadly. "Private. Do Not Disturb. Very nice, you two." There was something about that grin that said he wasn't going to budge. His hand was out, palm upwards. I rummaged in my pocket, and found a few coppers. He didn't look down, but weighed them in his palm. He stayed put, grinning. I dug deeper and got out some silver. "Good friends," he said. "We like you." And instead of that fixed grin he smiled.

I followed Claire through the narrow passage. "Thanks," she said, businesslike. "Let's find that lamp." As soon as it was lit she was ferreting through the clothes, her back to me.

"After *what*?" I said again. "You said you could handle VI easily … after what, Claire?" She straightened up suddenly, with something in her hands.

"Not now," she said. "Look the other way."

I haven't told you yet what Claire's style was, what kind of clothes she wore. That's not surprising. If I say she dressed in no style, I don't mean you'd have noticed her and said "that's gross". She dressed so that you wouldn't see her. Sarah, she'd be trying to wear what the in-crowd wore, just a month or two late and looking as if she didn't really believe the girl inside the clothes was her. Claire wore nondescript jeans and sweatshirts on the floppy side, so she could vanish inside them. I sneaked a glance after a while, and she was crouched in front of the mirror she'd unearthed amongst the junk, staring into it, then at something in her hand, maybe a hand-mirror? No, of course, I should have guessed: it was a strip of photos – not the ones Sarah had done for her but new ones, from the booth.

Then she stood up and turned round, and I hardly knew her.

It wasn't the clothes, so much – though the leather jacket made a difference. That, cropped at the waist, with the tight black jeans gave her a shape, a hard outline, that I'd never seen before. But somehow her face had done the same – sort of condensed, as though her features had gone hard and clear. She looked at me steadily, straight on. "Well?" she said.

"Hey... A bit scary..." This was a tough kid, streetwise, who knew what she wanted and would get it any way she needed to. She held my gaze, practising. I was her first audience; that was why she'd asked me. Now and then something wavered: a shade of the old Claire crossed her face. Then she'd glance at the photo again.

"Right," she said. "I'm going out..."

"I'll come..."

"No, Jon, sorry. Alone. You get the others. Meet me later, back here, all of you."

"Hey, wait a minute..." This was too much. First I rush out in the middle of my supper, then she sends me packing when she's done with me, *and* gets me running errands. "Who's playing Dressing Up now?"

"This is different." She came up closer, so we faced each other over the lamp. The glare of it, up from below, gave her deep hollows round the eyes.

"This is real. It was a game when Sarah did the sacrifice thing – like her photos. She didn't do it properly, with blood, I mean. She cut a bit of her hair. Some sacrifice!"

"It's a part of her," I said lamely. "She's proud of her hair."

Claire snorted. "Hair! It's dead already. The thing about a sacrifice is: something's got to die. No wonder she came out looking like a Barbie doll."

"Claire..." There was something in her voice that was making me more and more uneasy. "You mustn't take all this too seriously."

"Why not?" she said with a small laugh. "What have I got to lose?"

There was something in her voice that was starting to scare me. "Those new photos. Can I see them?" She shook her head. "Claire, what have you been doing?"

She straightened up and walked past me, into the shadows. By the crack in the wall she turned, a black shadow herself. "Don't worry," she said, in a calm flat voice. "I didn't use anything big. Anyway, it was a gift. This stray cat, a black one, it had something in the garden. When I shooed it off, there was this mouse thing, squealing but it couldn't move. So you see ... it was a good deed really. Just putting it out of its misery."

I was imagining the next bit, and I didn't want

to. "Where, Claire? In the garden. Tell me that you did it in the garden, not—"

"In the photo booth? Of course. Else it wouldn't be a *sacrifice*, would it? You've got to do it right at the moment when the flash goes. Don't look at me like that, Jon."

"Claire, stop it. It's only a game."

"You don't believe that."

"This is getting crazy."

"No, just serious. Look." She slipped the photos out and held them, a little too close to my face. She hadn't drawn on them at all; she didn't need to. "It wasn't easy," she said. I could see that. There was one Claire wide-eyed, pale with fear … one wincing – not in pain, more like disgust.

"I had it in a plastic bag," she said. "It kept wriggling and squealing all the way there. I could feel it in my pocket."

"What did you do?"

"I hit it. It wouldn't keep still. I swung the bag against the glass. Look, you can see." The third exposure was a pale blur, with just a glimpse of her face behind it. Her mouth was open. The last frame was the face she was wearing now, hard, bright and bitter. She whipped them away.

"That's why I want them here when I get back," she said. "I want Denzil to know I'm serious. Not like Sarah. And I want to make quite sure *she* knows it too."

"Claire, where are you going?"

"Oh, out," she said, too lightly. "Just out. See you later." Then she was gone, slipped through the crack in the wall. A stray cat, I thought, a black one, and she'd gone out on the prowl.

10

Burning Brian

The paraffin flame flickered, going smoky. For the twentieth time, Denzil bent over it to fiddle with the wick. "*When* did she say she'd be back?" said Sarah.

"She didn't."

When Sarah had answered the phone, she'd been relieved. "I've been trying to ring her," she'd said. "I've been really worried, Jon. Is she OK?" What had I been supposed to say to that? I hadn't mentioned the mouse; Sarah always used to flap her hands about and go all girly about mice, even when we were small.

When I'd phoned Denzil, I'd told him. I could almost hear him smiling, nodding slowly. "Well," he'd said after a moment. "The show's back on the road. Let's go." So the three of us had hurried to the arches … two hours ago.

"Typical," said Sarah. "She doesn't think. Mum didn't like me coming out, anyway. If Claire gets me into trouble…" She was pulling at the ends of her hair, like she did years ago, as a little kid, when she was angry. "It's not as if I really like her. I got landed with her, because she was always getting left out. I don't need her. I could have lots of other friends. I…" Sarah stopped and looked suddenly up, and the flame gave a flicker. Standing by the curtain, just where I'd last seen her, was Claire.

"Party time," she said. She came into the light of the lamp and put down a bottle – not wine, something stronger – and a few bars of expensive chocolate and a tub of expensive ice cream. "Double choc delight," she said, peering at the label as if she hadn't looked before. "I think it's melted." Sarah was staring, first at the party hoard, then Claire. Claire unscrewed the bottle, took a swig and held it out to her.

"Aren't there glasses?" Sarah said. Claire laughed, and thrust it at Denzil, like a challenge. He took it with that smile of his, and drank. "Not poisoned, then," he said.

He passed it on to Sarah. She hesitated for a moment, then took it and drank. Claire watched as she did it, and smiled.

She was right about the ice cream. We had to drink that too.

"Thanks, Claire," said Sarah, on the third round of the bottle. "Friends again." And she gave Claire a hug.

"All this stuff," I said. "It must have cost a bit."

"I don't think so." It may have been the drink, or just tiredness, but that stray-cat look was fading. She looked and sounded vague and awkward; she was Claire again.

"What do you mean: *don't think so?*"

"I... I don't remember." There was a pause. "I just know I was back at the station and ... and it was ten o'clock, all of a sudden. I kind of remember seeing you earlier, Jon, and... And I had all this in a bag, in my hand."

"I've heard about people like you," said Denzil. "Got this thing about shopping..."

"No, no, not shopping. I looked in my purse. I hadn't spent any money."

"Claire! You didn't ... steal it, did you?" Sarah was wiping her mouth, as if she could wipe the stolen goods away. "If I'd known..."

"I told you," Claire said. "I *don't know*. And anyway – even if I did – it wasn't me." She looked small and limp again. She still had the leather on, but it was just a bit of junk. It didn't even seem to fit.

"I'd better go home." Sarah got up and turned to

the door, but there was somebody standing there, just inside the curtain. VI. I was getting to like that grin of his less each time I saw it. He walked straight over, picked up the bottle – he didn't even say "Excuse me" – and drained it in a single swig.

When I got home that night, I crept upstairs. I reached the landing fine, and then a floorboard creaked. Mum looked out of her door. "You and your father," she muttered. "One's as bad as the other." That's all. An hour later in my room I still couldn't sleep. I thought of the town with all its streets and precincts empty, and I was down there, walking through the window of an empty shop. It was expensive, I knew that, one of those exclusive places with quaint signs like *Bespoke Tailors*, but there were parcels waiting for me – a pile of gift-wrapped things like hat-boxes or the most special kinds of cake. I went straight to the changing room, pulled the curtain and began to open them. I reached into the first and felt it – I mustn't look yet – and slipped it on, then I opened my eyes. It looked back at me straight on, with two more of it in profile, from the three-sided mirror, and there it was, my brand new face, a perfect fit.

"He hasn't paid yet," came a voice from outside and I was fumbling it, ripping it off, and it hurt. Worse, I forgot to stop looking at the mirror and began to scream and scream as I saw what of course you'd see underneath if you peeled off a face.

There was a boy in Sarah's life. I hadn't known that; no one did. He didn't know much about it either, I guessed. They'd met on holiday a couple of years before. Since then she'd written him letters, and got back a postcard or two. "But look," she said, "it says *Love*. And I think that's a kiss. It is, isn't it?" This all came out next day at the station. Sarah had convened this meeting. She wanted all of us to come with her this time, to the booth, for a new set of photos. If anyone doubted it last time, *this* time she was going to do it seriously, as seriously as Claire. And unlike Claire, she'd have witnesses; she didn't have to do it secretly, alone.

Sarah had holiday snaps – a few with someone in the middle distance, out of focus, who might have been him. But there was one of them side by side, at the last-night disco on the beach. These, and his cards, and the stick of an ice lolly he had bought her, were in a pink plastic folder. *Brian!* it said on the outside, with a heart as the dot on the *i*.

"I know what you're thinking," she said. "But he was gorgeous, gorgeous. And that's..." She looked up for the first time. "That's why he's the sacrifice."

"Hey!" Claire let out a breath. "But how? Where does he live?"

Sarah gave her a sour look. "Not him, stupid. All

this!" She flicked the folder open. There were pages and pages, too, in her neat rounded handwriting in mauve ink. "I tore him out of my diary – every bit. I'm going to burn them. Don't laugh, Claire," she said. "This is … *everything*." She bit her lip and pushed inside the booth.

"God, that's pathetic," Claire said. She and I had stepped aside a little, to pretend we couldn't hear the sound of muffled sobbing. Denzil had stayed by the door of the facetaker, shielding it and standing guard. "Talk about wet," Claire whispered.

"She means it. Had you been carrying that mouse of yours round with you, every day, for two years?" I said. "Well, then!" Over on platform three, a big diesel was powering up. As the smeech of diesel drifted through the station, Denzil slipped his zippo lighter under the curtain. A bit of smoke wouldn't be noticed now.

The snapshot – him and her together – was the last thing. That was the real sacrifice. Inside, she gave a choked little "Ow!" and there was the first flash, and the next, the next, the next. She stumbled out, cradling her hand. "I burnt my finger," she said. I guessed she couldn't let go. But Sarah wasn't weeping, not at all.

When the photos slipped out Denzil moved straight to the slot and took them. "No," he said. "We won't look now."

"They're mine!" said Sarah fiercely.

"We'll do it differently this time," said Denzil. "One each. I've got the felt pens."

"What? I do the pictures."

"We're all in it together now," said Denzil. "After last night."

The four of us looked at each other, then at Sarah. Yes, we were accomplices. We knew what Claire had done. Sarah had had her chance to walk out; she could have gone straight home and told her parents or, worse, the police. But she hadn't. She'd taken the bottle. She'd accepted stolen goods. "I ... I'm not doing anything like Claire did," Sarah had said when she phoned me in the morning. "But it's my turn next."

"We're all in it together," said Denzil. "This time we draw one each, I shuffle, you pick one. Pure chance. That way no one can cheat. Not even me." Sometimes you had to like him. The way he smiled when he said that, you forgot the last time you were angry with him. You just thought: if I'm playing, I want him to be on my side in the game.

Back at the arches, in the wardrobe attic, he made us sit in a square. "We'll do this properly. Close your eyes," he said, and pressed one each in our hands. When I looked, I knew immediately who this Sarah-face would have to be. She was stiff and upright, with her face screwed up against a wisp of smoke, and in the bottom right corner was a glare of overexposure that had to be flame. I gave her a bit more smoke, and a stake, and a halo. Joan of Arc, that's who she had to be. I'm no artist, but the picture drew itself, just a few touches here and there, and it was how it had to be.

When Denzil took them back in he made a great show of not looking. He shuffled and spread them out, face down. Sarah looked at them, and she was trembling. "I can't," she said.

"OK," said Claire. "We could ask VI."

"No!" Sarah snatched up a photo. She looked. Looked twice. Laughed. Shook her head. "I can't," she said again.

"You can. We'll help you with the clothes." Claire was straining forward. "Show us."

Sarah hesitated, then slapped it face up on the table and covered her own face with her hands. She was shaking a little, and I couldn't tell whether she was laughing or crying or blushing or flushed with excitement. But when she looked up she was calm and ready, and the show was about to go on.

We were following the tick-tack of her high heels down the street. Where Sarah had learned to walk on heels like that, and walk with poise and swish, I'd no idea. Her mum wouldn't have let her within a mile of the kind of clothes she was wearing now. It was hard to tell what it would feel like – metal or plastic – that tight little dress in gold-look PVC. I almost wanted to touch but, no, for heaven's sake, this was Sarah, cousin Sarah. Or it was and it wasn't. It was a Sarah no one in the family had ever seen.

"You can't go out like that!" I'd said, back at the arches, but she could. She hadn't been listening, staring at the mirror as if there was no one in the world but her and her reflection. She'd dragged back her hair and looped it and fastened it up with a pin, glanced at the photo again, then started on the make-up. Carmine mouth, her eyes slanted Egyptian-style, green-shadowed... When she'd turned round, the three of us had gasped together. "Sarah! You can't go out like that." But she could.

Claire and I, we walked behind at twenty paces. Denzil was keeping up, just. Tick-tack went the high heels as if they had a motor in them, driving her. There were a couple of wolf-whistles before we passed the station. By the time we were in Hyde Street a car had veered by and blared its horn, two young blokes leaning and leering out of the back window. What they shouted out, I'm glad I didn't hear. Now there were people around us, dressed for a night out in this part of town, with its expensive restaurants and exclusive clubs and bars. Denzil and Claire and I were starting to look as out of place as her. Then Sarah vanished, just like that.

There was a hole in the wall, a small dark doorway and stairs leading down. The walls and floor were matt-black, like the inside of the camera in the photo booth. By the time we got to him, Denzil was already arguing. There were two men – a penguin-suited bouncer and another man, in security-guard uniform, so exactly like him that he could have been his twin. As Denzil raised his voice, the two men took a step and loomed above him. At one side, the security man had a mean Alsatian, growling, tethered to the wall.

"She's our friend. Jon's cousin," Denzil was saying. "We don't want to come in, honestly. Just fetch her. She ... she's not safe alone." A slow sneer spread across the bouncer's face. "Looks like she's doing fine to me," he said, and chuckled. The other raised one finger slowly, close to Denzil's nose, then pointed at a small discreet sign. *Members Only*, it said.

"She isn't a member," said Denzil.

"Management's discretion," said the first one, with gum-chewing slowness. Dangerous. "Beat it, kid," he said.

"You don't understand..." I don't know if Denzil thought they would act as slowly as they talked, but he moved towards the stairs. In a second they were round him, ramming him back against the wall. "Leave him alone!" Claire shrieked and leaped at them, flailing. As one of them turned to swat her aside, I hesitated just a moment, then I was past them. The dog howled and leaped at its chain. I felt the tug as something ripped my sweater, but it missed flesh by a whisker and the chain rattled tight. The dog fell back. Then I was running down stairs three steps at a time. I burst into the bar, into flickering lights, a throb of bass, a crush of bodies swaying. I knew, as if by instinct, where Sarah would be. At the bar there was a knot of men, all clustered round one spot, and yes, in the thick of it, glittering gold-metallic, stretching a bare arm as she perched on her high stool, was Sarah. One of the men, a real smoothie with a silk shirt open to the belly button, had an arm round her already, and Sarah was giggling.

It wasn't bravery, the next bit – more unstoppable momentum as I burst in through the door. I crashed right into them, splattering drinks in all directions, and before they all turned, worked out what had hit them and started shouting, I had Sarah by the hand and I was yanking her back to the door. "Hey," she giggled vaguely. "We're having a party…" The blokes from the bar were closing in now, looking deadly.

"Do you know how old she is?" I shouted. Not much hope that that would stop them. Then the door kicked open and the two bouncers came through, hard and fast. As they ploughed into the crowd there were fists and knees and curses everywhere. I ducked through the door, pulling Sarah with me, stumbling up the steps. As the fresh air hit us, she seemed to blink and come to a little. There were Denzil and Claire, looking battered but not broken. He grabbed Sarah's other hand, and we ran.

11

Man's Best Friend

Faces, pelting at me. Faces, like snow hitting a car windscreen, hitting it so hard you flinch, then next moment they've melted away. That's what it was like in that crowd, with the four of us running. People's faces would look up, startled, angry, as we tried to veer and miss them. I cannoned into a group. "Sorry!" I turned to mumble, reeling backwards into the next. Everyone was in the way.

"Oy, watch it!" came a voice behind me, then others were shouting. They must have thought we were thieves or something, joyriders who'd just dumped the car and ran. "That way!" people shouted, pointing after us, and there was the worst sound of all – the low *gruff, gruff* of a big dog, getting closer. It had to be the bouncer's brother's dog, the Alsatian, and he'd let it off its chain.

"Split up!" called Denzil; he and Sarah peeled away. In a second, I'd lost them. "Claire?" I called, but she was gone too. *Gruff, gruff...* It was closer. I glanced back but all I could see were angry faces turning. Was the man running with it, or had he set it loose to run? But it could only track one of us... With a sick drop of my stomach I realized: I was the one it had nearly got a bite of. It would have my scent.

Crowds, crowds... Just a moment earlier I was looking for the open, somewhere I could get into the clear and run. No hope in that, with a dog behind me. I needed all the crowd I could get, as many smells, as much confusion... Yes! I was on the edge of the pavement, with the traffic revving from the lights, and beyond it, like a deep pool I might just plunge into, was the station. I teetered a moment then leaped; there was a squeal of brakes and more shouting, but I was ducking and weaving, in front of a bus, behind a taxi, making a bike swerve – more cursing – then I was into the station, burrowing into the thick of the crowd.

I slowed a little. Everyone was jostling here, a crowd flowing in all directions, some on their way home late from work, some out for an evening in town. If I could just slow down enough to stop them pointing, shouting. Behind, there was a blare of horns; I imagined the dog dashing into the traffic – oh, if there could just be a thump and a howl, and no more barking. But a moment later it was there again, not far behind: *gruff, gruff*... And there was the rasping, gasping sound of my own breath.

The booth was there, waiting. I wasn't looking for it, I swear. I was running, blindly, and I hardly knew which way, and then it was there as if it had stepped out in front of me. Just outside was a cleaner's cart, with broom and shovel. I swerved, but not enough, and I tripped on the spade and went down on my knees.

For a moment the pain blanked everything, then I was struggling up, but the knee wouldn't hold me. I stumbled forward and caught myself against the booth, and pulled myself inside. I had the crazy thought that if I got my feet off the ground, the dog might miss me, but as I pulled myself up on the seat I heard it panting. It was there, outside, right now. I grabbed the only thing I could see, to fend it off, and there was the shovel in my hands, just as the dog's nose came thrusting in under the curtain. I saw its jaws half opened, and the black lips pulled back from the teeth, then I chopped down blindly. With a horrible yowl, it twisted sideways, and a spatter of bright blood sprayed from the gash in its head; it twisted back towards me, jaws wide now, and I slammed down again.

This time the shovel came down on its neck, just behind the flattened-back ears, in guillotine style. It rammed the dog's muzzle down into the floor, and it thrashed, pawing the air with all four legs at once, gave a rattling growl and slumped on to its side.

I shrank back, gasping. Any second now, the man would burst in through the curtain and he'd kill me, kill me just the way I'd killed his dog. I should have been running, but I was paralyzed. I should have been thinking, but my mind was noticing silly little things – the sign saying Eye Level, and In The Event Of A Problem Contact TruVue Photographic Services, and an address in Slough. Any moment now, the man…

But he didn't burst in. Outside, there were footsteps and chatter and an engine shrilled and the announcer's tannoy coughed and echoed, but no one was shouting at me, no feet were running, and here in the booth it was weirdly still. Then I saw just what I'd done, and where I'd done it. The facetaker. It was a sacrifice, the biggest we'd given it yet. You can say I was in shock if you like, and half out of my mind with adrenalin and panic, but I found my hand reaching into my pocket, and there were just the coins I needed. A pound, and a pound, and a fifty. What else could I do but feed them in the slot? It took them as if it was hungry. The red light came on; I looked up and there was my face in the glass, and *flash*. The blue-white light went through me like a shock. It pinned me back on my seat as if I was strapped in an electric chair. *Flash*. For a crazy moment it was as if the inside of my own skull *was* the camera – no, as if it was a darkened cinema and there was a tiny me in the back row, a kid who'd sneaked into an eighteen certificate film and found himself in there alone as the image of my own face flashed up on the screen, huge, with a vacant look and staring eyes.

Flash: there was a picture of the dog's jaws dripping as it lunged at me. *Flash* – the last one was brighter and for a moment I couldn't see anything. There was a smell of electrical scorching in the air. Then I blinked and realized where I was again.

Very cautiously, I peeped through the curtain. As if nothing had happened, crowds flowed to and fro. I eased myself out – my knee was working – and looked back. The dog lay like a full sack, next to the bloody shovel, on the floor.

Sometimes your instinct takes over. I pulled the cleaner's cart towards me, just enough to block the door. For a moment I thought: could I just get enough leverage, could I tip the dog in…? No way. It felt as heavy as a person, and I couldn't start to lift it. Still, I hinged up the lid and, as the smell of garbage hit me, threw the spade in, with something vague in my mind about fingerprints, and slammed it shut again. There was a *click!* behind me, and I looked round, to see the photos drop into the slot.

It was then that I knew what I'd done. Sick, sick, I thought. Yes, to lash out in self-defence – it was luck that I'd killed it – that was one thing. But the photographs? What had I done? What had it made me do, the facetaker? I should walk away and leave the photos there, not even touch them. But how could I? They were my face. Fingerprints are one thing, but who in their right mind leaves four snapshots of themselves at the scene of the crime?

They should go in the cart with the garbage. As I reached for them, I turned my head, not to look, and I was face to face with the girl on the advert, with her terrible big teeth (three or four more were inked out, since Denzil) and that pitiless smile. I had the strip in my hands now. I opened the lid of the cart. One glance, maybe, then I'd drop them in and walk away.

It was that one glance that did it. As my eyes met mine … and mine and mine, the noise of the station seemed to drop into the distance, like the sound in a sea shell, hushed and far away. There were three faces – the last frame was a scorched black nothing – and they were looking at me, desperate, asking for something. They were alive, I knew; to throw them in the cart would be to kill them; they'd never forgive me. I was in shock, like I said. You can blame anything on that. Or I could be truthful; in one part of my mind I was thinking: yes, so that's what it's like. What Claire must have felt, and

Sarah. It shows you yourself, the parts you hide deep in your skull till *Flash!* they're looking at you face to face.

I could have said *No* at that moment, but I didn't. I couldn't stop now. Even if I didn't know if I was playing the game or if the game was playing me, I knew it had to go on.

In the booth there was a rattling and the dog's hind leg began to shudder. It couldn't be still alive, not with that gash in the side of its head. Rigor mortis, I thought, but the dead thing's leg was drumming against the plastic, as if trying to send a message. Any moment someone would notice. I had to get out of here. I ducked back into the crowd, going anywhere but back to the entrance. My heart was rattling too, as rapid as the dog's leg on the plastic, and I wasn't sure that I was breathing, but the crowd seemed to part and close behind me. I was putting distance between myself and the booth. Just as I started to feel *It's OK, I've done it*, this shape loomed out in front of me and blocked my way.

VI... And he smiled his village-idiot grin.

"In a hurry," he said slowly. "You should say 'Excuse me'." Slowly he began to laugh, at his joke about himself, till his big slumped shoulders shuddered with it. I could almost feel the ground beneath us rocking with the weight of him laughing. VI was a big big man.

"I *am* in a hurry," I said. "Just let me—"

"The man with the dog," VI cut in. "Me and my brother, we saw him looking for you. We hope he doesn't catch you." He was looking at me now, not blinking. In the middle of that plate-shaped face, there was nothing halfwitted about those near-transparent glass-blue eyes.

"What do you want?" I said.

"Want?" said VI. "We're friends. Friends. Excuse me," and he reached out and lifted the photo booth strip from my hands.

"Friends," he said again thoughtfully. Then with quick movements of his clumsy-looking hands he ripped the strip in half and half again. Each of the torn off bits he ripped once more for luck and he tossed them aside, confetti. It was gone – all that, gone… For a moment I didn't know whether to shout at him or thank him, then I saw that he was smiling, smiling broadly, at something still cupped in his big hand.

He held up the last remaining photo. It was surprisingly neat, the way he'd torn it. Ragged-haired, wild-eyed, its face flattened by the light of the flash bulb, it stared back at me. Creepiest of all, the thing I hadn't noticed when I'd looked just now, the shock of it all had stretched my mouth wide in a frozen kind of smile.

VI clapped an arm around my shoulder, and I flinched, from the weight of the arm and the smell.

It wasn't that horrible tramp smell like Alice, but something creepier, like mould and mothballs. After all, the clothes he wore were new each day.

There was a clattering roar and a train slammed past, so the light of the windows flickered on his face and mine. VI raised his other hand to the dead-looking faces in the windows, and waved. When it was gone he held the photo up for me to see again.

"You," he said, with a wide smile. "Friend. Could be my brother. Look, you're just like me."

12

Over and Under

"Come with me." VI set off down the platform briskly. I'd never seen him like this. Mostly he hung round in the station just mingling – that, or he lurked, half underground, in his cave. When Mum was younger she worked in a psychiatric hospital for a while, and she used to say that the first thing you learned was how to walk so everybody knew you weren't a patient. Brisk and purposeful, she said. You had to look as if you had somewhere to go. I don't know if VI had been an in-patient, but he would have looked like one anywhere he went.

Not now, though. He looked like a man with somewhere to go. Where, though, I couldn't guess. This was platform seven, the furthest, where no trains seemed to stop except the occasional goods trains shunted for the night. A couple of orange lights made patches of half light down the platform but there were no benches, no waiting rooms, no monitor screens. Ten paces off he turned to see if I would follow. Beyond him the platform began to narrow as the lines on either side converged, then it sloped and was gone. He was leading me nowhere, and seemed to expect I'd want to go.

This makes it sound as though I was thinking. No, something inside me had started juddering, like a faulty circuit, back in that photo booth. One moment I was in there, with the dog's teeth snarling. Flash. Then I was outside, photos in my hand. Then there was VI and now I was following him along the platform, as if there was no option.

I looked back once. "Come with me," VI said as we set off. "The dog man's looking for you," Someone must have found the dog by now, and what would he do, the dog man? He might call the police; that would be bad enough. Or else he'd handle it himself, in his own way, him and his brother the bouncer and the kind of friends I guessed they'd have. What that might look like was a one-frame flicker, mixed up with a memory of blood and teeth and shovels, in the darkroom of my brain.

"Where are we going?" I said as I reached VI "There's no way out this way." Overhead there was a jolt and clatter, where a row of dangling hooks came trundling overhead, on the conveyor belt line that took mail bags across the tracks, towards the sorting office. When letters plop on to your doormat in the morning you don't stop to think that they've been out in the dark, on trains, in sacks hoisted like dead things on butchers' hooks, in heaps sorted by bleary people working through the night. VI didn't say a word, but just turned and strode on.

Off the end of the platform there was a steely glitter on the rails where they narrowed to the viaduct. Much further, they splayed out again and there was a red light or two, and a green. We walked off the end of the platform like stepping off the end of the world.

"We aren't allowed here," I said to VI's back, as our shoes crunched on the cinders. He skipped over the rails into the shadows where bushes crowded in. I followed, watching the ground for trailing brambles, cables, splashes of oil and thinking of the other muck that, thankfully, I couldn't see. I remembered a film about a boy who played on the tracks and got his foot caught in the points and couldn't get it out, and then a train was coming…

There was a hee-haw of an engine, muted, far away, and suddenly there was a train out of nowhere, no, out of the tunnel in the red-rock hillside just ahead. We pressed back into the bushes but it swayed on the branching of points and veered away, to pass on the far side, going into platform one. Still, there was a sputtering blue flash beneath its wheels, and the arc-light flash lit up our faces like lightning, or the photo booth again. Again I had that flash of a picture printed on the inside of my eye, and it was me, a self-portrait except that the body looked like mine but the face was VI's.

A little further on, he stopped. The railway land was narrowing in, and instead of the bushes was a shoulder-high brick wall. "Uh-oh." VI had stopped. "Uh-oh," he said again. I stepped up to look over where VI was leaning, and saw where we were – above the arches. I saw something else, like a punch to my stomach. Right beneath us, where the workshops were, there was a police car with its red and blue lights flashing. Wherever we were headed for, it couldn't be there.

"Over and Under," said VI "We'll do the Over and Under."

"Pardon?"

"The Over and Under. Where have you been living? You'll have to learn your way around, you know." With an impatient gesture of the hand he was striding out again, and by the time I drew level we were well out on the viaduct, the streetlights dropping away on the main road below.

"Won't anybody stop us?" I said. "Aren't we trespassing?" He gave me the shortest of looks, as if it had been a really stupid question. "Where are you taking me?" I said again.

"Safe place. I said: Over and Under. This is Over." He giggled. Then there was a clunk and a quivering sound in the rails beside us. "Uh-oh," he said again. "Quick march." It wasn't a long bridge, and the end was in sight, but so was the oncoming train. Head on, down a long stretch of straight track, it was far off, a small caterpillar's head of light, but it was getting larger as I watched. All of a sudden the gap between the brick wall and the rails seemed very narrow. VI had not stopped to stare, and I was right behind him. I don't think the driver could have seen us, but as he bore down on the bridge he loosed one of those two-tone blurting noises I heard most nights, floating up across the valley. From the safety of my attic I used to think it sounded sort of lost and far away. Right now, it was the bellow of a bull animal lowering its head to charge. I ran.

I don't know how long it was, but then there was nothing but running. The crunch of my feet on the gravel, the rasp of my breathing, my heart … and a playground chant, over and over. It was the rhythm I'd heard VI humming at the booth, that first time I went in.

> *Facetaker*
> *Facetaker*
> *Take her in and*
> *Snap her Break her*

Was that VI's voice ahead of me, or my voice in my head? I couldn't tell.

Facetaker
Pace maker
Faster faster
Heart acher…

In front of me, VI vanished; he came to the end of the wall and he threw himself sideways; I launched myself after him and for a moment the world was turning cartwheels. Something ripped at my clothes and tore my elbows and then I was slithering down the gritty slope. There was a high whine and a crash of noise above me; I glimpsed the thrash of wheels and pistons, a bright rip of sparks, and the steel bulk as high as a house. I felt the air suck at me in its slipstream. Then as suddenly as it had come, it was gone.

"My clothes," I said. Parts of me were stinging badly; I guessed there'd be blood, but thankfully it was too dark to see. "My clothes. They'll be ruined."

"Not to worry. Plenty more in Auntie's Wardrobe. Now for Under."

"Must we?"

"Oh yes. Unless you want to go back Over. To the dog man. No?" He was up on his feet; saggy-kneed, he went scree-running zigzag down until the bushes thickened. As I came to a stop beside him, everything was still. The bushes had closed in, thorns and brambles, and I couldn't see where the path could lead on. Then in the hush I heard a little slip-slop trickle, like a running stream. I looked where VI was looking and that's what it was, just at our feet … except that the water in the deep brick culvert was an oily seepage with a dustbin smell.

"Under," he said simply, and lowered himself into the culvert, on to a foot-wide ledge. Only when I arrived beside him did I see where Under was. At the arch where the stream vanished into its tunnel under the embankment they had put an iron grille. It was clogged up with twigs, matted grass and bits of refuse – there was a broken umbrella, a black bin-bag and a child's white sock, just one – but at the side it had been prised back. Cat-foot on the narrow ledge, VI led the way through.

Then there seemed to be no time at all. As I squeezed through that grille there was nothing but dark and that throat-wrenching smell and VI's voice in front of me saying now and then "Steady. Easy goes now, Steady." I went half a pace at a time, my right foot forward, feeling for the cracks and the slippery places. My hand was reaching up to find the wall, feeling for the bulges that could knock me out or knock me sideways. I didn't know how deep the water was or what was in it, and I didn't want to know. I reached out like a blind man, needing to touch the wall for safety, flinching when I did. There were cobwebs that clung to my skin, or fleshy root-hairs; there were small things that squirmed at a touch, or mouldy masses where my fingers sank in. I looked back, and knew at once I mustn't. The tiny hatch of light back there illuminated nothing, but it was twice as hard to turn back to the darkness when I had.

We went, half a pace at a time, until my neck and legs ached, and little sparklers of light were going off in the dark of my brain, and it felt as if all this had been going on for all the time there'd been so far and all the time there'd ever be.

It could have been five minutes or five hours before I was sure: yes, there was a slight glow ahead of us. And yes, our steps and the plip-plop of the drips in the water echoed differently; there was a hollow feeling and I knew the roof was higher overhead. The left wall pulled aside, too, and the ledge became a chamber, like an Underground platform with the orangeish glint on the water instead of the rails. At the same time there was a sharp smell in the air and, in the corners of the chamber now and then, a reddish glow. I thought of prehistoric burial mounds, with their side-chambers neatly stacked with bones, except here the bones were still dressed in their skin, in rags and blankets, some of them curled up huddled close to their smoky embers. One at least in each huddle was awake, on watch, and faces lifted in the firelight, gazing at us blankly as we went by. Gaunt faces, shaved heads, swollen battered faces in a stack of whiskers, faces that looked very young, girls Kate's age, faces like Egyptian mummies, they looked so old.

Don't stop, don't stare, said a voice in my head, though it could have been VI's. *Don't look back*, it said, and I didn't, though for one heart-stopping moment there was a face that I knew, I thought I knew, no, surely it couldn't be, no. Mr Pinkus? *Don't look back*. And suddenly VI straightened up and stretched his arms and we were through the portal, back outside with air to breathe and over our head the good familiar orange sky.

The park… Yes, as we scrambled up the muddy slope, out of the culvert, I saw where we were. Just over there was the path where Denzil and I had talked the other night, beside the river. Just somewhere dry to sit, to rest with my back against a wall, that was luxury, and as I got to the path I flopped down on it with a sigh.

Maybe I fell asleep for a moment. I'm told that's what homeless people do. You can't sleep nights when you're out in the open. You sleep on edge, with an ear out for danger, and you catnap in the day, so the one starts to blur into the other, and you spend your whole time on that misty edge of sleep. I came to. There was VI sitting next to me. He looked switched-off, but his eyes were open. And coming along the path towards us was a couple.

They didn't see us – they were arm in arm, wrapped up in each other – until they were too close to do anything but walk on by. "Excuse me…" VI started, by instinct, in his begging voice. The man pulled the woman closer to him and quickened their pace, but he couldn't help glancing at me as they went by.

He stopped. Fatal – he stopped and looked back, and I recognized him, and saw the moment when he stared, and stared again, and realized it was me. His face went white and his eyes flashed. *No! Don't speak!* they said.

He fumbled in his pocket. He came straight to me. Leaning close, he pressed the coins in my hand. "Taxi," he hissed. "Get yourself home, OK? We'll talk in the morning."

"Yes, Dad," I whispered, but he was turning away, steering the woman with him. I didn't recognize her. As I watched them walk away I felt VI watching me. He wasn't stupid, not at all. Behind those glassy eyes, his mind was working, figuring out quicker than I did what it was I'd seen.

13

Man to Man

I wanted to sleep in. I didn't want to open my eyes. I wanted to blink and find that last night wasn't true. But there were the clothes still crumpled underneath the bed. There was the smell.

I'd glanced at the clock and it was nine, then ten, then eleven. Someone tapped on the door. I buried my head in the duvet and turned over. If I could just drift back into that old dream in which everything was normal and right and slightly boring, that old dream called my family... Sometimes I dozed, and then the dreams I got were much too real – jumbled rushes from last night, with the dog, the train, the tunnel, and Dad's face again and again.

Then another time I was in the loft beneath the

arches, and there were two figures hunched across the table, with the light behind them so at first I couldn't see. Without taking his eyes off the other, one swept the dust from the table with his sleeve, and I knew it was VI; on the other side Denzil took up the cards and began to shuffle. He shuffled, shuffled in the silence with a sound like a butcher's cleaver cutting gristle and bone. Then he started to deal, as if for poker, and I was gripped by a feeling of dread. *But it's only a game,* I tried to say aloud. *It's not even for money.* No sound came from my lips. VI glanced at his cards, then back at Denzil, then he pushed his wager forward. I was right: it wasn't money, but something bigger, and before I could see what it was I heard my own voice start to scream…

The knock on the door was harder this time, and Mum called "Jon? Are you awake?" After a minute she gave a little hush of irritation and went away. I shut my eyes tight. Then Kate walked in without knocking.

"Come off it, Jon," she said. "You're not asleep. You've got to talk to Mum, you know."

"What about?"

"Oh, come on. It won't help to play stupid. You know." I opened my eyes. Kate was flaming. I might hate her, like brothers and sisters are meant to do, but she's got spirit, I must grant her that.

"Anyway," she said, "Sarah's parents phoned last night."

"What… What did they say?"

"Only that she went to some weird fancy dress party and came home looking like … well, Mum wouldn't say what Sarah's mum said. Only wearing high heels and an ankle chain and a dress so short it came to *here*!" Kate snatched the duvet off me. "And you act all innocent: *Who, me? Sarah* told her mum she was going out with you! God, what's that smell?"

"I … I fell in a ditch."

"Great. Really sordid. Some party. So you got drunk and Sarah… Jon, you've got to say something. Mum's livid. Apparently Sarah was in a real mess when she got home – floods of tears, and she won't tell anyone what happened."

I groaned. "I'd better phone her."

"Not unless you're crazy. Her mum'll kill you. She's convinced that it's something to do with you… Oh, and Sarah's not going *anywhere*. They've grounded her for … oh, for ever, I should think." There was a knock on the door, and Dad's voice. "You're in for it now," Kate whispered. As he opened the door, she scuttled past, and he closed it behind him carefully. He didn't explode. There was a long pause. We were looking at each other like two animals put in the same cage by mistake at the zoo.

"Your mother's very worried," he said, looking at the floor.

I bet she is, I thought. She should be. "What about, Dad?"

"Sarah's mother phoned. Did Kate tell you?" I nodded. "I … I agreed with your mother that I'd have a word with you. Man to man." He tried a sickly smile. "That party…" he said. "It must have been some kind of party… OK, you don't have to answer… Jon, I'm worried about you, too."

I bet you are, I thought, after what I saw. "Me? Why, Dad?"

"All right, let's get to the point. In the park last night… I saw the way you looked. You looked terrible. I really thought you were a down-and-out. And … your eyes. Jon, I've seen the videos, I've read the leaflets. You'd been taking drugs of some kind, hadn't you?"

"No!"

"Don't lie. It only makes things worse. We've seen other signs, too. Sneaking out late in the evening. Getting secretive. And someone said they saw you hanging round the station." I must have flinched at that, because he sat on the end of the bed. "Jon," he said, in a confidential kind of voice. "I know how it is. I was young in the seventies. You think: I'll try it once; it makes you feel good, sort of special. And all your friends are doing it too, and you think: it's OK, I can give it up any time I want to. But you can't. You get hooked."

He was looking at me hard now, as if we were

playing chess and he'd just seen mate in three. "And ... and the thing about drugs is that you can't think straight. You think you know what you're seeing but ... but you imagine things."

"Dad ... I know what I saw."

He took a deep breath. "Jon, she's just a friend from work. She was feeling a bit upset, and I..."

"Dad..."

You know when you have to swallow a really big tablet, and you aren't allowed to chew it. You have to take a mouthful of water with it, get it in the right position at the top of your throat, then just make yourself do it. Gulp. That's how Dad looked. "Jon, you're a sensible lad. I've always felt I could talk to you..." If he'd said *man to man* again I think I'd have thrown up. "I know what you must be thinking, but ... when you're older, you'll come to realize. All of us have ... other sides to us, things it's better not to talk about, just in case it ... hurts people, you know what I mean?"

"You mean..." I was piecing it together, slowly. "You mean if I don't say I saw you last night, you won't say you saw me?" I waited for him to explode. He didn't. "And..." I said. "And we'll leave Sarah out of it?"

I was holding my breath now. Dad looked very pale. "You kids today," he said. "You frighten me."

You might think I'd be pleased as he left and closed the door behind him. After all, I'd won the chess game, hadn't I? No way. *You're a sensible lad. I've always felt I could talk to you...* Who said I wanted that? I wanted him to tell me that I'd been mistaken. Right then, all I wanted was to wind us back a day, a week, to being a boring normal family, or seeming to be one, even if I knew, and he knew that I knew, it wasn't true.

There was a package on the doorstep. It was shapeless, bundled up in several poly-bags and string. The postman had been hours ago, and there were no stamps on it. It could have been something left out for a charity collection, except for the big childish letters thickly felt-penned on it. "Jon", it said.

Inside was a sweatshirt. It was almost like the one I'd ruined. If I ditched the old one quickly, even Mum might not notice the difference. The size was right, too; someone was very observant. Very. At the thought, a sick chill feeling rose up through my stomach. Holding the sweater up to my face I caught the slight old-mouldy smell of Auntie's Wardrobe. I threw the thing aside and ran back to the door, but of course there was no one in sight. I'd known there wouldn't be.

Dad was right about one thing, though he couldn't know it. Some things are addictive. You get hooked. I remembered our first turns with the Facetaker, how I'd said: *It's just a game.* That should have been it, but what had happened? Claire. Then Sarah. Then... I shivered at the thought of last night. I'd never planned to do that; I'd never do it again, no, never. I'd had my go – or rather, it had had its go with me. Now that was it. Finito.

Sarah wasn't telling, that was one thing. If Claire was going to snitch, she'd have done it by now. No, the Facetaker was still our secret, and that's the way it had to stay. I thought of Dad, his *things it's better not to talk about*. I felt sick to hear him saying it, but sometimes it was true.

VI, though... He knew. He knew everything. He even knew about Dad and *his* secret. It was quite a mask he wore; you took one look and thought: *the Village Idiot*. Oh yeah? And finding that parcel was the worst of all; it meant he knew something else too. He knew where I lived.

14

Reel to Reel

Then I was ill. The sick cold feeling that began to rise in my stomach the moment I saw VI's sweatshirt went on rising. I was dizzy and shivering. No need for excuses now; I was flat out in bed all that day and the next, as the smells of cooking drifted upstairs – Mum seemed to be cooking all the time, another family meal, the table set for her and Dad and Kate and Keir and me, all in our proper places – and I felt sick to the pit of my stomach. I closed my eyes and saw black water in the culvert, and the iron grille, the child's white sock, and the cabbagy smell of the tunnel seeped up from beneath the bed – though I'd buried the clothes deep in the dustbin – and it took me by the throat. I lay facing the wall wanting not to be awake and thinking, but afraid to sleep. When I let myself, I didn't like the dreams.

And where was Denzil? Why hadn't he called? Kate and Dad hadn't said anything about him. By the sound of it Sarah's mum hadn't either. The last time he saw me I was about to be torn apart by that Alsatian; you'd think that he might want to know. Each time the phone went I stiffened, listening, but it was always for Mum or for Kate. I could hear them; the walls of our house are like cardboard. I could hear it was never for me.

On the third day there was a ring at the doorbell, and I heard Mum's voice: "I'm sorry, you can't; he's ill…" I jumped out of bed and was halfway down the stairs before I saw who it was – not Denzil but Claire.

"I've seen her," Claire said when we were upstairs on our own. We were both talking quickly and low. The way Mum would be feeling now, I knew she couldn't help listening. If we were whispering, her ears would prick up: danger. And as for Kate… I used to tell her that it was pressing them to keyholes gave her such funny shaped ears.

"She just wants to make sure," Claire said, "you won't say a word about Denzil. Ever. Her parents don't know he was there. If they did, she says they wouldn't let her see him any more." She made a little clenched face. "There. She made me promise that I'd tell you."

"Thanks," I said. "Anyway, what about me? Why should I get all the blame?"

"That's different. You're family."

"Have you heard from him?" I said.

She stared at the window glumly. "No. But she hasn't, either," she added quickly. "*And* it's all her fault things went wrong. At least I took care of myself when I had my turn, didn't I?" I raised an eyebrow. "And I handled the police the other night," she said. "They saw me down by the arches, but I didn't tell them anything. They gave me the *Don't-let-us-see-you-again* routine."

"Claire…" I said. "We've got to stop it, this Facetaker thing."

"What?" She swung back as if I'd stung her. "Why? Just because Sarah messed up… Give it a week or two. We can't just *stop*. Jon, it's the most —" She struggled for a word — "the most *real* thing that's ever happened to me. Don't you believe that any more?"

"I didn't say that. I wish I could. It works. Don't you see: that's why we've got to…?"

She was shaking her head. "That night," she said. "My night. I've never felt like that before."

"I thought you couldn't remember."

"Well, bits of it. But I remember what it felt like. Sort of free. Like flying." Just for a moment the stray-cat look stole back across her face and I could see: maybe it always had been inside her. That's what the Facetaker showed. But it had been out in the open now, and it wouldn't go away.

"Aren't you scared?" I said. "You should be. Claire, it was only shoplifting last time … but the next? And what about the sacrifice?"

She shrugged. "Well, if Sarah can get away with burning a couple of stupid postcards…"

"Claire," I said. "Listen." And I told her all about the dog. I mean all of it – the blood, the gash in its head, the way its leg wouldn't stop twitching. Once I started I couldn't stop, though the sick feeling swept back and the bed swayed.

"Hey… Well done," she said.

"No! Don't say that." She was looking at me in a way she'd never done before. More the way she looked at Denzil. "No, Claire, we shouldn't be enjoying it. We've got to stop, before something really awful happens."

"But… Denzil…" She looked at me, suddenly big-eyed. "If we won't do it with him, he'll…. he'll find someone else."

"No," I said. "We've got to see that he doesn't. Claire… This might be the last chance…"

I thought she was going to fling off in a rage but no: her eyes narrowed. "You'd tell, wouldn't you?"

"If that's the only way to stop it…"

"Don't!"

"So we stop it ourselves. Together. That's the only way."

She was looking at me hard now. Then she gave a hopeless little sigh. "Great," she said glumly. "So who's going to tell him?"

"I will," I said. Somehow I didn't trust her to.

"Oh, by the way." She turned on the doorstep. "I've got something for you." I stared at the limp thing she'd plonked in my hand. It was an old tie, very wide and fraying at the edges. It was hideous – bright red, with big grinning cartoon dogs on it, Scooby Doo and Scrappy Doo.

"It was that creepy village idiot guy from the arches. He was there at the end of the street – just appeared out of nowhere and said: 'Excuse me...' He seemed to know I was coming to see you. Jon, you're shivering again. You should get back to bed."

"What did he say?"

"Nothing, really. Just looked at me and let that stupid smile of his go frozen, you know how he does. And when I walked away he just stood there like a statue, watching. Then when I looked next he was gone." I guess I could have told her all about VI, and that night, and the Over and Under, but I felt so tired and sick. Not now, I thought, not now.

She frowned. "Jon, I'm worried. I mean: the tie... I know you've got bad taste, but... He said it belonged to you."

It was like being a little kid again. Now Mum and Dad could say that I was ill, it sort of wrapped up that night and the whole Sarah thing. Maybe they thought being ill was a punishment and now I'd learned my lesson. Mum started being nice and bringing me up boiled eggs and hot Ribena. I'd take them and say "Thank you", and inside I was feeling six years old again, except I wasn't. When I was six I thought you could believe what parents said. When they said *Kiss it better. There! It's all right now*, it was.

And when I fell asleep I dreamed of running. I was outside, on the viaduct, looking down on the town with its lights and little houses like a toy place, and I was like the cats and foxes, wild things that stalked the streets by night. I had wide eyes like them, all alert and twitchy, ready to hunt or be hunted. Half awake, I found myself thinking: could I run away? I wondered if I'd dreamed Over and Under, and if that could really have been Mr Pinkus. If I sat beside his fire, would he recognize me, and what would we say?

The phone rang. Rang and rang. It dawned on me slowly that the house was empty. Everyone was out. I dragged myself out on the landing and, "Hello?" said the phone when I picked it up. "Jon?"

"Denzil! Where are you? Where've you been? What's—?"

"Cool it, Jon, and listen. Something's happened."

"You bet something's happened. I nearly got

eaten alive, Claire nearly got arrested, Sarah's locked up by her parents. Denzil, we're not playing any more."

"We?"

"We talked it over, Claire and me."

"Mmmm. That's not what she said when I saw her last night. But Jon, listen, none of that's important now…"

"You bet it's important."

"Jon," he interrupted. "Jon, I've seen her."

"Who? Sarah?"

He made an impatient little *huh*. "I mean *her*, Jon. *Her*. The one this has all been about, except I didn't know it. Suddenly it all makes sense. Pin back your ears and listen." I sank back against the wall and listened. He was on full power, a hundred words a minute. What else could I do?

He'd been browsing through the racks in Reel To Reel, the new video shop just off the High Street. There was this little window through at the back of the counter, into some kind of office, and there it was – that face, that lovely dark neat face with the sharp little corners to the eyes and lips. It was framed in the small square hatch exactly as it had been framed in those four photos. Yes, it was her – the face from the photo booth, the one we found the day that Alice…

"Hang on," I said. "Are you saying that's it. She's real, and all that stuff about Alice – her secret self, her alter ego, doppelgänger, whatever you said – all that … it's just not true."

"No! It's true all right," said Denzil. "You know the Facetaker works. It shows us things – things about ourselves. You saw Claire, and Sarah. And you've been there too, from what Claire tells me. You can't doubt it now."

"So what about this girl?"

"Mona, that's her name. Mona. We were meant to find her. Those first photos were a message."

"Who from?"

"Oh … don't be so *pedantic*. Some things are just *meant*. And anyway…" He was improvising; I could tell. "What if it shows us the future? Claire's face, the Stray Cat, that came true, didn't it? Well, what if it was showing that Mona's the future for me?"

He'd gone back to Reel To Reel later in the day, and the next morning, and the afternoon. He looked through New Releases, then through Horror, Thrillers, Adult, even Family Entertainment, and all the time he had one eye on that window, for the moments when her face would be framed. He listened, too, as the people at the counter chatted – they were film bores, of course, but when they thought there was nobody in they grumbled a bit about the hours and the wages, and the boss. Denzil started to pick up names. Mona. Then this middle-aged guy in a jacket and tie and a gold watch, with a bald patch and a thin moustache, came out and looked round, and the lad at the counter called him "Mr Griffiths" and Denzil realized that the reason he looked as if he owned the place was because he did. Then the man said something about staying in town tomorrow for a meeting, and could they make sure there was a taxi booked to take Mrs Griffiths to the station at 6.45. At that moment Mona came out of the back room and – I could hear Denzil swallow hard before he said it – then the man slipped his big fat arm around her waist.

"Do you know what that means?" said Denzil. There was a buzzing silence down the phone. "What it means is: she's married. She can't be more than eighteen. I've been out with girls of eighteen. And she's married to an old guy in his forties. Isn't that gross? This middle-aged fat guy who owns a video shop. She's married to him. Isn't that obscene?"

"Well, that's that, then." I breathed a sigh of relief.

"No! It's just going to be harder to get to her. I'll need help, that's all." It was when he said *help* that the sick feeling came back. I took a breath.

"So you've fallen for her. Bad luck. Love, that's all it is."

"No. Not just love. Fate. She's what the whole game's been about. We never realized – probably weren't meant to."

"Denzil, this is crazy…"

"Alice – she was incidental. She was just the sacrifice. I haven't figured it out; I just know all this was meant to bring Mona to me… I mean, us," he added quickly.

"Us? Count me out," I said.

Silence.

"Count me out," I said again. "We're all in bad enough trouble as it is. And there's something else – VI. He knows."

"Knows what?"

"Everything. He's seen us all. He saw Claire's stolen stuff; he saw Sarah; he knows about me and the dog and … and other things."

"Things?" said Denzil.

"Family things," I said. "Don't ask." I should have known: tell Denzil *Don't ask* and he will. He listened as I told him, then he laughed.

"What's funny?" I said.

"Do you know," he said, "how many affairs my dad's had? And my mother. They've got an arrangement. Simple!" When we met first I used to wonder what kind of parents they could be, to have a son like Denzil. They sounded cool. I used to wish I had parents like that, whoever they were. Since the other evening, I wasn't so sure.

"He could do a lot of damage. And he knows it."

Denzil gave a little snort of laughter. "Him? Oh, come on. Criminal mastermind, is he?"

"He's not stupid. He knows where I live. And he's making sure that I know that he knows."

Denzil wasn't laughing any more. "Let's get this straight. Do you mean blackmail? What does he want? How much?"

"I don't know." It might just have been that I was sitting on the landing in pyjamas, but suddenly I shivered. *Goose walked on your grave*, my grandmother used to say. What if it wasn't money that VI was after?

Denzil didn't speak for a while, then "OK," he said. "No problem. Leave it to me."

"What are you going to do?"

"I'll have a word with him. I'll fix it. Trust me? Good. And in return, you can help me."

"Help you?" I said, as if I didn't already know.

"One more go with the Facetaker. Fair's fair, Jon. I haven't had my turn yet. Just this one last time, for me."

15

Silent Movies

I was back in the loft at the arches. *No,* I thought, *no, please not that…* But it was: the game of poker. There was Denzil, who looked at his hand, keeping it tight to his chest. VI's back was towards me, leaning over, so I couldn't see the stakes between them, but I could see that knowing little smile on Denzil's face. *I'll raise you,* he mouthed, without sound, and pushed something forward, and though I knew I shouldn't look how could I resist? Then I was screaming again, as I always did these days, in dreams like this, because the wager was a human face. I would have said *death-mask,* except that it was alive, its eyes wide and its lips open in a silent scream. As you'll have guessed, the face was mine.

* * *

It was a relief to be back at the till at KwikSave. Keep the trolleys rolling, I thought, keep the dog food coming – anything rather than have time to stop and think. But I was tired and fumbling. Crash: that was the third thing I'd dropped since lunchtime, a jumbo family saver bottle of tomato ketchup this time, and I watched in dreamlike fascination as it splattered like B-movie gore. The shopper was turning round, her hands raised, like a footballer appealing to the ref ... and the manager was striding over. "What's got into you?" he started. There was more but I didn't hear it because there behind his shoulder in the plate glass window, pressed up to the glass, was a face that I knew. It was Denzil. He huffed on the window and drew in a circle with a snarl and big round glasses, like the manager's, and he stood behind it wagging his finger just like the manager. I couldn't help it; I began to smile.

"If that's your attitude," said the manager, "you can go."

"I'm sorry." I tried to pull my face together. "I'm not very well. I only came back to work this morning."

"Not very well! I've never liked your attitude," he said. "There are people queuing up for jobs like this. You can take your cards and go." Behind him, Denzil made the glasses into big bloodshot eyes and sketched on a couple of horns in a rough imitation of the Jack of Ghouls. I cracked up laughing. I could go! That was the best thing I'd heard for days, and I punched a final five million pounds on the end of the bill, got up and walked away.

"Right. Listen hard," said Denzil outside. He was walking fast. He wasn't laughing any more. "I talked to VI. I thought we could do business. You're right. That guy's a problem."

"What happened?"

"He said *No*."

"*No?*"

"No. There he is begging for small change every day, and I offer him real money and the guy says no."

We sat down on a bench at the edge of the square. Why there, I didn't ask. Denzil had decided; that was that. Pigeons started circling in and landing, pecking like clockwork at the sandwich crumbs and litter round our feet. "I took him at his word," said Denzil. "You know his line about his brother and his train fare home. Well, you offer him a cup of tea and he's happy. So I thought: why not offer him his train fare home? Wherever that is. I don't care. Twice over, if he likes, for his famous brother…"

"Sounds like a lot of money," I said.

"Don't worry about that. Remember the Stray Cat? Our little cat-burglar shoplifting friend…"

"Claire wouldn't…"

"Who knows…?" He raised his eyebrows. "Maybe Claire would do it specially for you… We all want that creep off our backs. Or have you changed your mind since yesterday?"

I thought of Dad's face, in the park, when our eyes met … and VI watching. Just observing, as Denzil used to say. I thought of VI lurking at the end of the street, waiting. No, I hadn't changed my mind. "So?"

Denzil kicked a polystyrene cup and half a dozen pigeons wheeled up, clacking their wings in thirty seconds's panic, then dropped down again. "So I offered him his fare twice over, and the guy just grinned at me. 'No deal,' he said. 'You want more?' I said. 'How much?' He just grinned harder. 'We don't want your money,' he said. 'Jon's my friend.' And he laughed in my face." The tight smile Denzil gave was nothing to do with humour. "Well you may shudder. He wants something else."

What had VI said that night? *Friend. Could be my brother. Look, you're just like me…*

"I wonder what happened to his brother?" I said. "If he had one."

"Oh," said Denzil. "Didn't you know? Maybe better not…"

"What?" I had that crawling feeling in my stomach.

"It's only a rumour," said Denzil.

"What? Tell me."

"If you say so… They say… They say there were two of them. Twins. And there was some kind of accident, on the railway line. They say that's why he went … like he is."

I shut my eyes, and I was on the cinder slope at the end of the viaduct looking up into that crash of noise and oil and steel. "There," said Denzil. "I thought you'd rather not know."

"Oh my God," I said, "he thinks that I'm his brother. Denzil, he needs help."

"He needs getting rid of. Don't look like that. You said it yourself, he could do a lot of harm, could VI. Not just to the four of us – your family… Wouldn't you like to see him gone?"

"Yes, but…"

"Jon, be rational. What's wrong? Who needs him? Who would miss him?" Out on the road there was a squeal of brakes, and the pigeons burst up in a fluster round us. "Who missed Alice?" He gave a little chuckle to himself. "He's always saying that he wants to go home to his brother. Well…"

"Well what?"

"Look!" said Denzil abruptly. I looked where he was pointing, just across the square, and I saw the sign above the window: Reel To Reel. So that's why we'd sat here. "There she is!" If I hadn't known otherwise, I'd have thought she was a picture, or one of those almost-life-size cardboard cut-outs video shops stand in their windows, she was so still.

As still as in the photos, that small perfect face gazed out, just gazed. "Come on. This is it," said Denzil, and we were heading over there, as fast as you can pretend to stroll. Not that she would have noticed us. Wherever her mind was, it was miles away.

He pushed open the door. "Excuse me," said Denzil. He had his charm voice on, but it wavered a little, as if he was breathless. "I'm doing a PhD on silent movies. I need some specialist help…" She had turned when he spoke, startled, and frozen like that, with her eyes gone slightly wider, her lips slightly apart. That look on its own would have been enough to stop me in mid-sentence. If she was lovely even in the photographs, the real thing was not to be compared. She was little and delicate, I could say doll-like except for the warm apricot tinge to her skin. She was something that didn't belong here in England, and she was perfect. Even Denzil, Denzil the actor, faltered. I'd never heard him dry up in mid-speech before. Then I saw why. Out from behind Family Entertainment came the husband. "Is that him?" he said back to the counter, then he brought his face down close to Denzil's. "They tell me you've been hanging around."

"I… I'm a film buff," said Denzil, lamely.

"Really. Who was the female lead in Valentino's first film? Or just the title? Just the year?"

"What is this," Denzil tried to laugh a little. "Trivial Pursuit?"

The man pulled back his lips from tobacco-stained teeth. Then he glanced at Mona and made a slight movement of his hand towards the office. Without a word, she lowered her eyes and went. "I don't want kids hanging round this shop, OK?" the man said. "Run off home, boyos."

Denzil was off across the square in long strides. I could only just keep up. "Right…" he muttered. "Right, that's it." His lips were drawn up very tight and pale. I knew what it was; he'd just been laughed at for the second time that day. "Don't take any notice…" I tried. "He's just a—"

"Shut up." He looked up, with a sort of cold fire blazing in his eyes. "Right," he said again, and something in the way he said it made me shudder. A moment before he had been taut and quivering, as if he could snap. Now he was suddenly spookily calm. "Tonight," he said. "I know which train she's catching. An hour with her, that's all I need. If I can just *talk* to her…"

"Hold on, you don't know anything about her. She mightn't even *like* you."

"She will," he cut in. "I can do it, with a bit of help."

"From me?"

"From the Facetaker. Jon, remember the Ace of Guys…?" I did: suave, sophisticated, like James

149

Bond, Dracula and the Count of Monte Cristo all rolled into one. Denzil looked at me hard. I'd made a *maybe* sort of noise. "I can be him," he said. "If the Facetaker works, the Ace of Guys is *me…*"

I opened my mouth. "Leave it," he said sharply. Then his face relaxed into that slow smile. "I said I'd fix it. I'll fix it. OK? Two birds. Meet us at six."

"Where?"

"At the booth, of course." He turned on his heel and strode off fast across the square, his long coat flapping.

I stood there staring after him. Then I had that feeling, the cold prickling feeling you get in your back when someone's watching you. I looked round and at first I didn't see. Then, yes, over by the junction, where the crowd was waiting for the lights to change, there VI was standing. Just observing. He was looking directly towards me. The next moment, the green man flashed and the crowd moved. By the time they'd cleared, he was gone.

16

Magnolia Park

It would be all right. It was going to be all right. I kept saying the words to myself like a mantra, meaningless words to soothe the nerves and still the brain. Denzil knew what he was doing. I could trust him. He'd know what to do with VI.

I knew that look in his eyes. It meant that he had a plan. But what? What did he mean: *that guy needs getting rid of*? What did he mean: *I'll fix it*? What did he mean: *two birds*? I told you how Denzil used to drop a word in out of nowhere, and when he'd got you interested he'd explain … maybe, in his own time. Six o'clock this evening he'd explain everything, and it would be all right. All I had to do was pass the time till then.

I was walking, and I didn't know where. It just

seemed better to be moving. I looked up at the corner and saw where I was – Hyde Street. What if the club was open? What if the bouncer was there, looked out and saw me and…? Don't even think of it. I spun round and set off the other way, as people ploughed into me and swore. The other way, then… No, I'd be back at the station, and my stomach gave a lurch at the thought of the booth. The dog. The smell of rubbish. And I knew, just knew, that somewhere VI would be watching. Perhaps he was watching me now. For a wild moment I thought: I could corner him, I could pick him up by the frayed lapels of his smelly old jacket and shake him: *What do you want? What will it take to make you leave us alone?* I could imagine my voice as I did it, and it wasn't threatening; it was pleading. Please please please, it was saying, just vanish. Let me forget all this. Let's say it never happened.

Somehow I knew, too, that I'd never find him – at least, not if I tried to. When I didn't want him, he'd be somewhere, glimpsed from the corner of my eye, all the time.

But Denzil would fix it. When I saw him at six, he'd say: it's OK, I've fixed VI. End of story. I could just go home and … I'd be home with the family, as if nothing had ever happened … except that I would always know it had. And the family? I'd seen things I couldn't un-see. No, it would not be the end of the story.

What had Denzil meant: *I'll fix it*?

Just walk, Jon, walk, I thought. Somewhere. Say the mantra. But I couldn't. Down in my gut I knew that it was not, not, *not* all right.

"Jon! What's the matter with you?" I blinked and there she was. Sarah. "Aren't you meant to be at work?"

"I'm OK," I said faintly. Somewhere in the background a dog barked, and I flinched.

"You look terrible…" She glanced round quickly. "Mum'll be here in a minute. She mustn't see us. Oh, there she is…" And she gave me a small push, and before I knew it I was walking. Later I thought: another minute, and I'd have told her, I'd have told her everything. Maybe if I had, things would have been different. But I was walking, and I knew where I was going now – to Denzil's house.

Magnolia Park. I'd never been there. Denzil never said, "Come back to my house"; that wasn't his style. It was hard to imagine him at home, or having parents. You thought of Denzil, you saw him out and striding somewhere, going where he wanted to. I'd seen the name of the street on some parents' letter from school, and thought it sounded posh. Maybe that was why he'd never asked me back.

"Magnolia Park?" I asked in the post office. The little man behind the glass did it all by hand signals: up the hill, turn right, turn right again. The last gesture seemed to mean Straight On, For A Long Time. Quite how far I didn't realize until I was there and walking, past the last estate and right out to the edge of town. The weather-bitten sign, Welco to Ma oli ark, appeared at the roadside, as if out of nowhere.

There's nothing there: that's what I thought, faced by a line of trees, dull dark straight-up firs planted close to make a hedge. No roofs and chimneys above them. For a moment I could have believed that even his address was made up, another of Denzil's bits of play-acting. Then I peered through a gap in the trees and there was Magnolia Park – not a close of exclusive mansions but a square plot with half a dozen caravans on concrete standings, and a few cars pulled up between them. I suppose it would have called itself a mobile-home park, though these homes hadn't been mobile for years. They were jacked up on little brick pediments where the wheels had been. Some had little tacky fences in between, and even gardens, with flowers in rows and here and there a plastic gnome.

Outside one, a young bloke had a large black motorbike stripped down to a skeleton, with pieces scattered round him, bleeding pools of oil. "Pardon me," I said. "I'm looking for the Hunts." He raised his hairy head and squinted. "Denzil's place…" I said. He lifted his huge monkey wrench and pointed.

154

To be fair to them, some of the mobile homes were as big as a small house. With their creamish walls and dulled chrome trim all round, they made me think for an uneasy moment of the photo booth, but stretched to twenty times its size. They'd have two or three breeze block steps up to a door with a name and a knocker. In the furthest corner of the field, beyond the last of them, tucked in round the back of a rickety shed, was a small green caravan with wheels but no tyres. That was the one the biker meant; there was no mistaking it.

At the door, I knocked – just a tap, but I felt the whole wall tremble. I knocked twice, and there was no reply. So that was it: I was in the middle of nowhere, and no one at home. I had no idea what I was doing here.

I looked at the caravan. It was not much bigger than my bedroom. How could a family live in it? I peered in through the window. There was a table, and a tiny basin. There was one mug on the washboard, one plate on the rack. It might have been true, the things that Denzil said about his parents. If so, their flexible "arrangement" meant that neither of them was living here.

How did he do it? How could anyone just … live alone? Instead of a house, next door was a tumbledown shed with ropes of cobweb in the window and a glimpse of ancient tins of stuff that only sixty-year-old gardeners would know.

Gromore. Paraquat. I thought of the nights I'd lain in bed and fumed at my family – at Kate's snide comments, Keir's spoilt-brat whinging in the night, and Mum, and Dad – times I'd heard the hooters of the night trains and wished I could be miles away. But not like this.

Through the caravan's smeary window I could see a door through to a second room – half-open, but from this angle I couldn't see through. And I had to. One more glance at the biker – he'd forgotten me, head down among the bones of his machine. I pushed through the long grass and weeds, to the back of the van.

"Denzil…! Oh…!" The voice changed in mid breath. "Jon. What are you doing here?"

At the back, out of sight, looking like a cornered animal, was Claire. She turned from the window with a guilty start. "Same as you, by the look of it," I said.

"Sorry," she said, "I thought—"

"You thought I was Denzil. Well, sorry to disappoint you. Again." We looked at each other awkwardly. "I thought you said you weren't going to see him any more."

"Well, maybe I'm not," said Claire in a choked voice. "Not now I've seen. Jon, did you know about … all this?" I pressed my face close to the glass where she was pointing, and I saw.

Once when we went on holiday to Greece my

parents took me round this old Orthodox church. There were holy pictures – icons, the faces of saints – staring at us on every wall. There was only the light of some flickering candles but every pair of saint's eyes seemed to be looking straight at me, and when I moved they followed me. That's how it was in Denzil's bedroom, which was a kind of shrine, I suppose, in its way … except that instead of the saints he had Monas. Big ones, blown up blurry photocopied versions of those four little photo booth snapshots gazed from the walls, the bedside table, the same face again and again.

On the bedside table, there were his photos too. There was the Ace of Guys, blown up to life size, propped up by his mirror, as if he was practising. Rehearsing. And there was another of it, photocopied next to Mona's, like the perfect couple. *Creepy. Claustrophobic* – those were the words that came to me. For the first time ever, I'd had a glimpse of the inside of Denzil's mind … and I wanted to get out.

"I … I didn't know," I said.

"But," Claire said, "surely she isn't real?"

"She is. Her name is Mona."

"Jon!" Claire glared at me. "You never told me. You mean … all this time." So I told her, as well as I could.

Claire stared at the ground. I wished I could help her, but I couldn't. Some dream of hers, about

Denzil, was crumbling in her fingers as she stood.

"Jon, I've got a really bad feeling," she said quietly. "Really bad. He's obsessed. He could do anything – you know Denzil…" She closed her eyes. "Two birds. Oh my God…"

"What?"

"*What?* Think, Jon. Two birds with one stone. He says he'll get the village idiot off your back. And he's crazy, I mean really crazy, about this … this Mona. I don't know what he's going to do with her, but he wants to be the Ace of Guys. He wants to do the Facetaker thing. *One last time. The big one.* Well, then… He's going to need a sacrifice. A really big one. VI – don't you see?"

We both stared through the window, noses pressed against the glass like hungry orphans outside in the storm. Perfect, perfectly impassive, Mona's lovely face stared back. She didn't know a thing about us, or any of this. She didn't know what horrible things he was planning to do for her sake.

"We've got to find him," Claire said. "We've got to do this together, Jon. Whatever Denzil's going to do, we've got to stop him, haven't we?"

17

Rush Hour

5.30... We'd started off running, Claire and I, but we'd soon dropped down to scout's pace – run a bit, walk a bit, run a bit again. It seemed even further back into town than going out. We were both panting, our lungs hurting with it, but there was no question of stopping. We both knew that we had to get back to the station before ... whatever. We didn't stop to discuss what *whatever* might be. We ran, and as I ran there was that stupid rhythm – it couldn't be VI's voice; it must be mine now – in my brain.

> *Facetaker*
> *Facetaker*
> *Take her in and*
> *Snap her Break her*

The further we ran, the weirder it got.

> *Earth shaker*
> *Moon raker*
> *Auntie's dead but*
> *You can wake her…*

What was I saying? No, keep your mind on your feet. Don't listen to your brain, I thought. Just run.

Meet us at six. That's what Denzil had said, the exact words. And he'd meant it exactly. It seemed like just the way you say it round here – *meet us …* means the same as *meet me…* Teachers always tell us off for it. But Denzil meant *us*. It was him and … who else could it be but VI he'd have with him at the booth?

5.45… I came panting up the steps towards the station, and paused. Claire was ten paces behind, but coming gamely, with her face blotched pink with effort. "Are we in time?" she gasped between breaths. 5.50… Yes, we must be. We just had to catch Denzil or VI before they met. We just had to make sure that it never happened.

"I'll look out for Denzil," Claire said. "You look out for VI. Oh yes…" She must have seen the look on my face. "You're supposed to be his friend."

"Stay in sight," I called as we stepped on to the concourse, into the height of the rush hour, the noise of the trains, the announcements and voices and the clash of luggage trolleys and the scuffling of a thousand feet.

I ploughed into the crowd. It was true: when I wanted to find VI, I couldn't. Near the entrance was his usual pitch. No sign of him there. I turned round for Claire, but the crowd had closed between us and she could be anywhere. "Claire!" I could hardly hear my voice myself. 5.55, said the big clock over the Departures. I forged on through the melee towards the photo booth. One of them might be early, or if we couldn't intercept them on the way, somehow we'd have to do it there.

"Jon!" Claire had reached the place before me.

"Any luck...?" I began, but something in her face told me no. Or something worse.

"Jon, look!" And I looked where she was pointing, at the corner where the Facetaker stood ... and saw. It wasn't there.

"What—?"

"I don't know!" Claire shouted. There was a rectangular mark on the pavement, a tidemark of grime, that showed where it had been. There was a bunch of black cables hacked off crudely near the ground.

"It's OK, then," I shouted. "If it's gone, they can't have..."

"No," she said. "Not OK. Why aren't *they* here – either of them? Jon, if they've gone somewhere with each other... We've got to find them before it's too late."

"The Arches!" I said, and we dived back into the

rush hour crowd together, jostling with elbows, knees and shoulders, jabbed by briefcases, handbags and umbrellas, fighting our way back towards the entrance as the evening crowd poured in.

Round the corner, on the back-road, it was suddenly still. Above us, the station rattled and hissed and rumbled like a huge machine, but down by the arches was a pool of quiet. An unsettling quiet. The thing with dark pools is you never know how deep they might be.

At the entrance of the lowest arch, VI's cave, we stopped and looked at each other. There was no sound in there, no light, nothing. "Come on," Claire said. "We've got to go in. Together, OK?"

Five paces, ten paces, slowly … we went into the darkness. Once she flinched and caught at my hand, but it was only a blanket underneath our feet. It was only the smallest of gasps she gave, but we might as well have rung a doorbell. "OK," I said out loud. "Is there anyone in there? Denzil? VI?" Each name echoed for a moment in the musty air.

"We're coming in." I said it as firmly as I could, but it quavered. "Don't do anything silly."

"Here's the back wall," Claire whispered, quite close. "Nobody here, unless … unless they're next door."

"OK," I said. I felt around on the ground until I found something – only a chair leg, by the feel of it, pinched from a skip, I'd guess, and half charred on the fire. Holding it like a small cudgel, I lowered my head, checked once for Claire behind me, and crept into the secret passage.

"Listen!" Claire's voice was scarcely a whisper. I was still holding the curtain open, as she ducked through and straightened up beneath my arm.

"What is it?" Frozen, I held my breath and heard it – a faint and hollow tinkling in the air. Suddenly she stifled a giggle, that was half laugh and half fear.

"Coat hangers!" she whispered. We relaxed a little. No one was in here, unless they were lying very, very low. Though that was a bad thought, and I shivered. "Find the lamp," said Claire.

It was in the usual place. That was reassuring. My fingers found the box of matches. They were damp, but on the third attempt one flared. For a moment I stiffened as the first glow of the lamp showed human figures, headless women or men with weirdly short legs that didn't reach the ground – just clothes on hangers. There was the same old stuff around us – Auntie's Wardrobe – but…

"Someone's been here," said Claire.

No wonder the hangers had been rattling. Someone had pulled out several of the rails-on-wheels and half-emptied them, draping the outfits here and there and everywhere. There had been a serious fitting session going on, with formal suits and long gowns. Then I looked beside the mirror, on the floor.

There were two faces, blown up to life size, Mona's and Denzil's as the Ace of Guys – the same as in the caravan. Remember those cut-out figures you used to get on cereal packets; you could try them out with sets of cardboard clothes? I had a vision of Denzil moving among these racks, among costumes that were almost like people but lacked faces, and trying them with his face or Mona's. I could see him dressing Cinderella and Prince Charming for the ball.

"Too late," said Claire. "Let's go back to the station. It's giving me the creeps, being here."

"The photo booth…" I had a hunch. "Wherever it's gone, that's where they'll be."

The woman in the canteen didn't recognize me straight away. That's how it's always been with me and Denzil. No one forgets him, but me… "The photo booth…" I said. "What's happened to it?"

"Oh, the workmen took it away. There was an electrical fault the other day. It nearly started a fire. People kept trying to use it, so they got a fork-lift truck…"

"Where? Where did they take it?" said Claire.

At her voice the manageress's eyes refocussed and took us both in. "Oh," she said starchily. "I knew I'd seen you before…"

"Please," I said. "I left … something important in it."

"Hmmmm." She adjusted her glasses. "Platform

seven, I think. I suppose you know your friend was here asking the same question." Halfway out of the door, Claire came back as if jerked on a string.

"As a matter of fact," said the manageress, "I noticed him particularly. I was thinking he'd taken a turn for the better – buying one of those down-and-outs a cup of tea. Then he spoiled it." She fixed us with a look. "You might think it an act of kindness giving these people strong drink; it only encourages them."

I glanced at Claire. There was a question in her eyes I couldn't fathom. "Strong drink?" she said. "Tea?"

"Oh, he might have thought no one was looking, hiding himself in the corner, but not much escapes me, in *my* buffet. Before he took the tea out, your friend poured a wee dram of something in it." Claire looked at me. "Well may you look surprised. Shame on him. And the big man drank it in one go."

The crowds still buzzed behind us, but as we stepped on to platform seven there was an empty feeling in the air. The hooks of the mail-bag hoist hung empty overhead. There were the same lamps, lighting nothing but some empty trolleys. I stood and looked up and down the platform, feeling hopeless. Then there was Claire's voice, from behind a pillar. "Jon! Over here!"

At first I didn't recognize what I was seeing, at

that angle. It was lying flat, where the workmen must have dumped it, with its blank back upwards and the entrance on the ground. If it hadn't been for the poster panel on the end, it could have been any old grey flat surface. Except it wasn't quite flat. One corner, the corner furthest from us as we looked at it, was slightly raised, as if something was trapped under it.

"Uhhhh..." Claire gave a shudder. "Jon...!"

Poking out from underneath the corner of the booth were the four pink tips of what I suddenly realized were the fingers of a hand.

18

The Big One

We looked at each other, Claire and I, and if either of us had turned to run, the other would have too. Claire spoke first. "We can't just leave it. Help me." And we were struggling to shift the fallen booth. It was hard – there was something heavy in it, but the plastic walls would bend and nearly crack, and then when you let go they'd spring back. "Wait a minute," I said and scoured around to find a lever. Yes, there was a metal bar, and once we'd forced the end underneath we both heaved on it and, yes… With a creak and a shudder the booth flipped on to its side, leaving VI, crouched up like a foetus, lying crumpled on the floor.

"Is … is he dead?" said Claire in a small voice.

"I think so."

"How can you tell?"

We both bent as close as we dared. There was the usual mouldy smell about him, but something else too. There were no marks to his face or his head, and no blood, but around his lips there was a kind of frothy spit that made me wince.

"Jon," said Claire. "Remember what the woman in the buffet said?" She was looking beside the body, at the polystyrene cup the wind was rolling to and fro. "What do you know about poison?"

"Nothing. Denzil wouldn't. I mean, where would he...? Oh God, no..." I was back at the caravan park, with the abandoned shed next door. *Paraquat.* Now I knew where I'd heard that name before. Years ago, on the news, when they said they'd banned a weed killer after several not-so-accidental deaths.

"Why?" she said. "Why would he? I mean, it isn't even plugged in? There are no photos."

"The sacrifice... Maybe he thought that's all that counted, in the end."

"Uhhh!" Claire gave a sort of whimper. "Jon ... his hand! You said he was dead." And I watched as the first fingers of his left hand twitched, as if beckoning. I thought of the dog, how its leg had started to twitch, and twitch, and twitch...

"Quick," she said. "Help me turn him over." VI felt heavy and clammy through his clothes, a sack of damp earth. "On his side," she said. "If it's poison, we should make him sick."

"How?"

"Stick your fingers down his throat, I think."

"No!"

"OK," she said, eyes blazing. "I'm not scared. Uhhh... Ah!" She jumped back as the mass of VI heaved, then coughed, then with a rumbling choke began to vomit horribly in a stinking puddle at our feet. His eyelids flickered and for a moment there were only white balls, with his eyes rolled up. Then he was looking at us, wrinkling his forehead in a frown.

"You..." he slurred.

"Don't talk. We'll get an ambulance."

"No!" He was struggling up on one elbow. "No ambulance. They took Auntie away. Not me." He frowned harder as his eyes rested on me.

"You..." he said. "Your friend... He said you'd be here to meet me. Said he'd take our pictures, you and me. Like brothers. I feel bad. Bad..." His eyebrows knotted with the effort of bringing something back to mind. "He tricked me," he said. "Bad tea. Made me poorly. Bad!" He wrenched himself up to sitting, and fell back against the side of the booth. It creaked. "Where is he?" The words were an ominous rumble now, a growl from his gut. "Where *is* he?"

"We don't know," I said. Claire was backing off, mouthing: Run, Jon, Run, Jon, Run, Jon. Now!

"Where IS he? Wanna *talk* to him!" VI gave a

heave and staggered up; for a moment his legs held him, then gave way and he collapsed into the wreckage of the booth. As plastic splintered around him, he roared, "Wanna *TALK* to him…"

"Run!" said Claire out loud, and her voice broke my spell. We sprinted for the lights and hubbub of the station crowd, that had never seemed so comforting before.

"The train about to depart from platform six is the 6.45 for Midgely." High up in the iron rafters, the announcer's voice was a rattling cough. "Stand clear of the doors please."

6.45… "Claire!" I caught hold of her sleeve. "That's her train. Mona's. That's where he'll be." We ducked past the barrier and ran, zigzagging between people, as the carriage doors shut, clunk, clunk, one by one. I grabbed for the last one just as the guard put his hand to it, and held it open as Claire scrambled in. We fell into a crush of sweaty harassed people, standing room only, grumbling at us as a whistle blew; the train lurched and juddered into motion as we pushed our way on through.

"Are you sure she's here?"

"Sure? Of course I'm not sure!" I ducked beneath the armpits of a mountain in shirtsleeves, and out into the space between carriages. "If she is, you bet she'll be in First Class…" I glanced out of the window. We were pulling down the platform – no turning back now. And all at once there on the dim-lit platform opposite, not ten yards away, was a shape I knew – VI. He was scanning the train, window by window. Then suddenly he was staring straight at something – someone – a carriage or two forward, not at me. As the train gathered speed he had turned and was running with it, jogging then loping in long strides, keeping pace. I could see his mouth was open, shouting, but I couldn't – didn't want to – hear.

So Denzil was on the train. Him and Mona.

The whole length of platform seven, VI kept up. Once he had to leap an empty trolley, but he took it in one bound, without taking his eyes off the train. As he ran, in the half light, he seemed to stretch longer, grow bigger, and I saw just how much his beggar's hunch and shuffle was an act. He was pounding along now, losing ground slowly as the train gathered speed, and his face, his mouth wide open silently shouting as he ran, would be in my dreams, coming after me, not giving up, for a long time to come.

Then suddenly there were no lights and no platform. I pressed to the window to see if he was teetering, stopped, on the end of platform seven, but I'd lost him. I remembered that night he'd skipped over the tracks while I was stumbling. But he could never catch us now. I turned back to Claire. "Let's find Denzil," I said.

Now we were under way, the rush-hour crush had settled somehow, and we could push our way through the second carriage, and the third. Then suddenly there was space, and we were in the blue plush ambience and leg-room of First Class. There were empty seats here. And, halfway down the compartment, there was Denzil, too.

He was smart, I'll give him that. He'd made full use of Auntie's Wardrobe, and he was a living image of the Ace of Guys. He looked the part from head to toe, and had the manner – casual, suave, masterful. He was talking, with his face towards Mona, who sat perfectly upright, rigid, in the same print dress from before. I guessed if I looked at his feet I'd see the bag he'd brought her clothes in, new finery from the Wardrobe, but I couldn't take my eyes off the paralyzed look, the rising panic, in her wide dark eyes.

He looked up, and he saw us. There was a cold flash – *Don't say a word! Don't know me!* – in his eyes, but it was too late for that now. "It's OK," I called. "VI's all right. It's going to be OK…"

But it wasn't.

There was a jolt and a squeal of brakes and with a kind of sigh the train slowed, slowed and came to a stop. I looked out. No, it wasn't a station. We were just beyond the viaduct, where the tracks and sidings opened out, and I could see the red light of the signal that had stopped us. Any moment it would go orange, then green. But it didn't. It stayed red. And somewhere behind us, VI would be coming with that long stride, loping down the line.

19

The Ace of Guys

After the din of rush hour, the crush on the train, the racket of wheels on the rails, the long squeal of brakes, it was suddenly still, with just a creak and click like metal cooling. Commuters glanced out the window vacantly, then folded themselves back inside their Evening News. "Denzil," I said. "This is mad. We've got to talk."

"I don't know who you are," said Denzil with complete assurance. "You must be mistaking me for someone else." It was a clipped voice speaking, one used to travelling First Class, quite at home in the smart clothes he wore. Even the way he moved his head was different, with the kind of look that would bring waiters scurrying in expensive restaurants, and not a word said. For a moment I actually thought he might be right and I was wrong ... but no, there was that funny older-looking face of Denzil's and, even more unmistakable, there was Mona at his side.

She was rigid and quivering. The lush honeyish tone of her cheeks had gone yellowish pale. Claire was glaring at her, looking fierce and tousled. Claire was going to hate her, this perfect exotic doll-face who'd captivated Denzil; she would hate her if she could. But Claire let out a breath and shook her head. "Poor thing," she said. "You're terrified." Claire crouched down close to her. "Who *are* you?"

"Pliss..." said the girl in a whisper. "No Ingliss... Sorry, pliss..." Her fathomless eyes went wider as they met Claire's. "I wish this man not talk... My husband... He come angry... Send me back." And she began to cry.

You've read the kind of story in the papers, and you've seen them on TV: how a middle-aged bloke, kind of sad but with a bit of money, takes a plane to Thailand or the Philippines. Sometimes they don't bother with the plane but get a catalogue with photos, through an agency, by post. What's wrong with that? they say when they're interviewed. It's not illegal. What kind of life would these girls have out there, anyway, in a village? And what true-blooded bloke wouldn't like a wife like that, let's be honest now? Doesn't answer back, does what she's told? Poor Mona, or whatever her real name was, in the language she'd left back home.

"Poor thing," said Claire again, and for a second I wished that somehow all this could be true. Of course it had just been coincidence, Denzil finding her photos in the slot at the booth. They hadn't been damp; he'd made that up, for the sake of the story, and we swallowed it, me and Claire and Sarah, because oh, we wanted something special to be true.

Did he believe his stories? Who knows? Just then, on the train, I wished he could be real, this suave and well-heeled Ace of Guys, and not just Denzil improvising. I wished he could whisk her away from this life she'd been sold to, the slob in the video shop. Maybe it was a photo in a brochure landed her here in the first place; I wished it could be a photo that rescued her now. That's what I thought, just for a second...

Then there was the thump on the window, and a glimpse of pounding fists, and the face – VI's – inches away, its mouth wide open, snarling. Mona screamed. The face fell back, then came scrabbling up, couldn't get a grip, fell back again. Denzil was frozen in shock, and he'd seen him. Two or three times the fists and face heaved up and the window frame shuddered. Then he was gone. Nothing. And I realized: he was making for a door.

"Get out!" said Claire. She was cradling Mona,

who'd folded up into her arms and was weeping, as small as a child. "Denzil, run. He'll kill you." He shook himself once and the Ace of Guys was gone – he was just Denzil standing there, uncertain, in his stolen clothes. He looked up the aisle, and down it. Which way had VI gone? Which door would he burst through?

Then there was a scream and voices raised just outside the compartment, and the automatic door slid halfway open, and there was VI squeezing the mass of him through it, forcing it back with a shuddering hiss. His voice came in a breathless bellow: "Wanna TALK to you…!"

By the time he was moving, Denzil was gone. VI crashed down the aisle in long strides, and was out of the other door, after him, leaving just a waft of his stale smell and fresh sweat. I pressed my nose to the window just in time to see Denzil vault from the door, land awkwardly on the loose gravel and stagger, then set off like a lame hurdler over the tracks. A moment later, VI was there too.

"He'll kill him," Claire whispered again. I was already on my feet. "No, Jon…!" she said, but I wasn't listening. I wasn't thinking. All I knew was that if anyone could stop what was going to happen, it was me.

Beyond the viaduct, the tracks splayed wide. There were branch lines from small stations up and down the valley, intersecting from both sides. There were sidings, some with rows of empty waggons, some with skip-like low-loaders heaped with gravel or scrap metal. There were goods lines hardly used, gone dull and rusty; there were the glittering rails of the main line, polished every hour by tons of steel. There were tangles of points where side-lines slanted in to meet or not quite meet, curved like scimitar blades. Beyond all this was the red rock cutting and the black eye of the tunnel, and the signal lights. A red, a red, a red. A green.

Denzil was losing ground quickly. The dips between the rails were deep, and his bad landing had hobbled him. The sleepers were greasy with oil, too; he slipped and went down. He was struggling up straight away, but VI was taking the rails each in a single stride, as if he did this every day. I couldn't keep up. So I did what I could: I shouted.

"No!" He didn't turn. I couldn't shout "*VI*". How come I'd never asked his name? "Friends!" I yelled.

That stopped him. In mid-stride, he teetered and looked round. "Friends?" I yelled again. For a moment VI hesitated, looking back at me, and on at Denzil, then in two bounds he had crossed the ground between them and had Denzil by the collar, lifting him and shaking him in both hands.

"No!" I hollered, stumbling closer. "Brothers!"

VI let Denzil fall to the ground. One hand stayed clamped on his arm, though, and didn't let go.

"Uh?" VI roared at me. "What do you mean – brothers?"

"All of us... You – me – Denzil... We're all brothers."

"Uh?" he said again, and his fist must have tightened, because Denzil gave a yelp of pain. "Say it again," said VI, craning forward. "Can't hear."

I stepped over the last track but one. "I said: Br—"

With a leap VI was over the line, Denzil dragging behind him, and his big hand swiped down on my wrist so tight I thought the bones would crack. "Tricked you, eh?" he said "Not so stupid as you think!"

He looked from me to Denzil, back to me again. Slowly his lips came back from his teeth, as though there was a joke he did not get yet, but he would. "Brothers...?" he said. "One ... two ... three ... No, only ever *two* brothers."

That's when Denzil seized his chance. "Yes!" he gasped. "Only two real brothers. I'm your brother, not him. He's lying. Don't you recognize me?"

You could say: that was it, at last, the moment when I saw what had always been true. Denzil didn't care about me. Maybe he'd never really cared about anyone – never had the chance to learn what caring even means. We'd been useful to him, Sarah, Claire and I, as he shifted from game to game – an improviser, like I said – as smoothly as shuffling cards. What was he playing for? How could he ever win? And if he ever tried to stop, how lost would he be?

I could almost feel sorry for him, when I think that. Right then, all I could think was: I'm disposable. Useful, if he needed one more sacrifice.

There was a kind of high-pitched hum around us, less a sound than a quivering vibration in the air. There was a hiss to it too, like the swishing of a huge fine-bladed sword.

"It's me!" yelled Denzil. "I'm the real one." VI gripped us, one in each hand. Slowly he held us out at arm's length so he could get a good long look, at Denzil's face, at mine… There was the blast of a hooter, muffled at first, then suddenly louder as the train burst from the tunnel. I could see it over VI's shoulder, and there was the driver's cab, and I guess he might have seen us because the hooter blared again, much louder, and the brakes began to scream.

VI looked from Denzil back to me. His hands were quivering as he pulled me in towards him, closer, inch by inch, till our noses almost touched. "You!" he whispered, very softly. "You…" And with a shot-putter's thrust he straightened his arm and flung me backwards.

Then I was turning in mid-air, with a freeze-frame glimpse of VI's face, and Denzil's, and another of the other train behind us with its hundred dull commuters staring out, and among them was Claire's pressed to the glass, aghast, and cradled in her arms not Mona but the puffed and blotchy face of Alice, and not weeping but lit up, laughing, laughing. Somewhere in my mind the one word echoed: *sacrifice*.

The gravel hit me, and I threw my arms up round my head, as if that could somehow fend off hurtling tons of steel. There was a clash and a roar like a huge dog jumping at its chain, and a slam of hard air knocked my breath out, though I might have been screaming, and the small calm voice in my head said: *Oh, so this is what it's like, to die? So this is it?*

Then I opened my eyes and there was the vision of it, raging high above me, like one long punch from one long fist of steel. Right here by my head there was pummelling dark, the flash of wheels and pistons, too fast to make sense of. Think of how a blender blade would look if you brought it up slowly, on full power, closer, closer, to half an inch from your eye.

But it wasn't me. I was watching. I could see it. The train was on the next track, where Denzil and VI had been.

Think of blender blades, all of a sudden and yet going on for ever. Or try not to think of it. Try. Try not to think of it when you wake up in the small hours, gasping for breath. Try not to think of it in every little crack between your thoughts at school, at home, at work, at rest, in dreams. Try not to think of it now, for the rest of your life, like me.

There's always one somewhere, in the corner of a crowded precinct. And it's always waiting, night and day. In the dark, it glows with its own cold light, from inside, behind the small curtains, like the moment when the house lights go down and everyone hushes as the film's about to begin.

There's always one somewhere, just out of sight. People are drawn back to it, again and again, to see what face it will show them, the Facetaker.

You've got to look. You must, although you know you won't like what you'll see.

MILLS & BOON®

Why shop at millsandboon.co.uk?

Each year, thousands of romance readers find their perfect read at millsandboon.co.uk. That's because we're passionate about bringing you the very best romantic fiction. Here are some of the advantages of shopping at www.millsandboon.co.uk:

* **Get new books first**—you'll be able to buy your favourite books one month before they hit the shops

* **Get exclusive discounts**—you'll also be able to buy our specially created monthly collections, with up to 50% off the RRP

* **Find your favourite authors**—latest news, interviews and new releases for all your favourite authors and series on our website, plus ideas for what to try next

* **Join in**—once you've bought your favourite books, don't forget to register with us to rate, review and join in the discussions

Visit **www.millsandboon.co.uk** for all this and more today!